I0517261

Secret Sins:
Murder in the
Church

Kathy Bobo

DEDICATION

To all the wonderful teachers I've had throughout my life and to my mother, Carolyn Howard.

ACKNOWLEDGMENTS

First and foremost, I would like to thank the one
that made this book possible, God.

PROLOGUE

Spirit Temple Pentecostal Christian Church has everything a good bible thumping Holy Roller would want, shouting, speaking in unknown tongues, Holy Ghost dancing, fainting and rolling around on the floor in fits of rapture, live music along with a fabulous choir. But it also filled to abundance with everything you do not want, such as; power, sex, betrayal, but the secrets are their primary keys to power and influence. Membership has reached seven thousand, so there will be four different services to accommodate the enormous congregation. Easter morning service, and that means it will be very long, and they still have to come back for Evening Service. Evening services can last past 2 A.M. seven days a week. Sunday school is at 8 A.M. and church services start at 9:30 A.M.

It is 10:30 A.M and the Ushers are wearing white dresses. Sister Nadine Dalton is a stately woman of seventy with salt and pepper gray hair, and she hands the collection plate to a woman sitting at the end of the pew and she passes it to the person sitting next to her. This routine continued for about twenty minutes until they completed the ritual, and that's with almost thirty ushers. Some people dropped cash into the collection plate while other dropped a collection envelope into the gold plate. This was not Nadine's Sunday, but the regular usher was helping someone that got over-heated and passed out, so the Mother of the Church, Mother Beulah Murdock asked Nadine to help. Nadine hands the empty tray to a young woman at the end of the pew, but when she got to the end of the last row. She noticed an opened collection envelope on the top, and sticking part of the way out of a tithing envelope, a lottery ticket. On perfect musical queue the ushers marched in to the beat of the music to the end of the church to a waiting Mother Beulah with their collection plates. Nadine whispers to Mother Beulah, "Someone put a lottery ticket in the collection plate."

Shocked, Mother Beulah demanded to know, "Who did it?"

"There are so many people…I don't know," answers Nadine.

Mother Beulah t e l l s Nadine, "It'll be okay. I'll throw it away in the counting room."

Nadine shot Beulah a questioning look, but remained silent.

CHAPTER 1

Shawn

The incident was anything but a gift from God, and we will soon learn not all gifts come from God, and I'll leave it at that.

It happened after Sunday morning church service. The finance committee of Spirits Temple Pentecostal Christian Church gathered as normal to count the money from the morning collection. On the finance committee is Assistant Pastor and Junkyard Prophet Reverend Alvin Carney, President of the Broad of Stewards and Vice President of the Board of Stewards, Melvin Sims. Jason Brennan, President of the Board of Trustees.

Treasurer, Nichelle Graves, Deacon Ray Murdock, and representing the Board of Deacons and Deacon in training Tyrone Lane, My mother-in-law, the mother of the church, Mother Beulah Murdock and Myself. Everyone had a pile in front of them counting the contents when Deacon Murdock takes a lottery ticket out of his collection pile. In the past we have gotten all kinds of things in the collection piles, IOU's and prayer requests, but never a lottery ticket.

Deacon Murdock has a bucket of cash in front of him, but instead of counting, he is reading the newspaper. Mother Beulah, "Put that paper down and count that money in front of you."Ray folds the newspaper and lays it to the left of him and pours the bucket of cash onto the table. Cash in various denominations flow from the bucket and coins rolls across the table. Ray gets things settled, he starts separating the bills by

3

denomination. Ray handles the cash in his hand like a professional banker, and counts just as quick. Ray likes all the heads going in the same direction, and he pauses and looks at a lottery ticket buried in the pile of cash in his hand. "Um…A lottery ticket," says Ray.

Nichelle looks at the ticket in Rays hand across the table, "Give me the ticket and I'll put it in the trash," demands Nichelle.

Ray starts to pass the ticket to Tyrone, but looks at the

ticket again, "Saturday, April 7th, 2012…this is for last night's drawing."

Ray opens the newspaper. In a obvious flippant attempt, Tyrone exclaims, "Just pass the ticket to Nichelle and she'll throw it away."

Ray jumps out of his chair and does a Holy Ghost dance and he begins shouting and speaking in tongues, "We've got a winner!" Everyone stops counting and looks at Deacon Murdock dancing with a ticket in his hand.

Shawn demands to know, "What's the meaning at this?"

Deacon Murdock hands Shawn the ticket and he looks at the newspaper and sure enough was a winner. A winning ticket worth One Billion Dollars and even Shawn gets into the spirit, "PRAISE THE LORD!"

When everyone else in the room found out, they began shouting and jumping for joy with sheer insanity. All were happy but, Nichelle. She urges everyone to calm down. Deacon Murdock grabs his daughter Nichelle and shouts, "This ticket is worth a cool One Billion Dollars, and we're not calming down anyway soon!" Deacon Murdock releases Nichelle, and informs her, "Can you imagine what everyone can do with their share of the money?"

Nichelle calmly sits down in her seat, crosses her legs, and says, "This church belongs to Shawn, everything in this church belongs to Shawn, including the collection." She couldn't wait to tell everyone in the room, "None of you are entitled to one red cent."

The room fell into a deathly silence and Ray staggered in disbelief and releases Nichelle. Everyone gave Nichelle dirty, angry looks including her father, "I didn't raise you to be selfish."

Junkyard Prophet says, "Amen there's enough for everyone to enjoy God's blessing and live happily ever after!" Junkyard continued loading currency into the counting machine and said, "Can I get a Amen!"

Mother Beulah with a bitter and angry expression on her face points her finger at Shawn and tells him, "This is the work of the Devil, and we need to find out who this ticket belongs to and give it back to them!"

Dismissively, Junkyard Prophet says, "Let's not call the Devil a no account dirty, stinking, no good..."

Tyrone Lane cuts off Junkyard before he has the chance to really get into saying something unsuitable in a church. Tyrone leans forward in his chair with a serious expression on his face looks at Mother Beulah, and tells her, "You're right and this ticket spells trouble and we need to get it out of the church."

Deacon Murdock approach's Shawn and starts to take the ticket from Shawn and says, "Know problem, I'll take it home with me."

Junkyard Prophet is a few inches short of being seven feet tall and three hundred and fifty pounds rises to his feet, "You'd better not touch him or that ticket!"

With a height of five feet six inches and one hundred twenty pounds, he looks up at Junkyard with a bit of trepidation, "I'm not some punk pastor. I can knock you on your butt!"

At first everyone stares and some people burst into a nervous laughter while others get angry, and Mother Beulah rises from her chair with her finger pointed at Deacon Murdock, "Ray, that evil ticket is not coming anywhere near my house!"

Deacon Murdock gets angry, but with a smile, "Women should remain silent in the church and even though you're my wife, I run that house not you!"

Shawn urges them, "Calm down, and for now I'll hold on to the ticket."

Tyrone Lane is the Director of the State Lottery Commission, and he tells everyone, "The IRS will hit an individual winner pretty hard in taxes, but if the church cashed in the ticket it would be tax free."

Everyone listens carefully at Tyrone, but it's Junkyard Prophet that breaks the silence, "Well damn! What'd you do? Rig the freaking lottery?"

Tyrone only glared at him without a response. Shawn takes the ticket from Deacon Murdock opens the safe after Nichelle's revelation ripped the joy from everyone's spirit and left it tattered into shreds on the counting room table. Shawn places the ticket in the safe locks the door, he asks the question, "Why someone would put a winning lottery ticket worth One Billion Dollars in a church collection plate?"

GUESS WHAT HAPPENS NEXT

CHAPTER 2

Junkyard Prophet

WHAT HAVE I GOTTEN MYSELF INTO?

I drove onto the parking lot and seen a truck from Murdock Construction parked on the front parking lot. Everybody has a key to the church but me and to tell you the truth, I don't want a key. In my opinion, to many people have keys around this church. I looked around the empty parking lot as I get out of the car. I was about to light a cigarette when Jason Brennan speeded onto the parking lot and jumped out of the car in a cheerful tone, "Good Morning Reverend Carney."

I smiled at Jason and say, "Now listen boy, I've told you a thousand times to call be Junkyard Prophet."

Jason gives me a quick smile, "Yes Sir…Mr. Junkyard."

Suspecting that was the best I was going to ever get from Jason I decide not to press him any further because Shawn was pulling onto the parking lot at that moment.

The three of us are walking to the front door as Jason walked to the front door of the church. Shawn glances around the parking lot as we are walking up the stairway toward the front door. I door turned the doorknob and it was locked. "I guess Deacon Murdock locked the door after he went in?"

Rev. Graves takes his keys out of his pocket and unlocks the door and all three go in to a dark church. Jason flips the light switch on the wall and the church lights up. Reverend Graves says, "Let's get this over with. I have sermons to prepare for the Religious Convention that starts Friday Night."

Jason said, "I've been looking forward to this all summer."

The Religious Convention was a big deal because Spirit Temple Pentecostal Christian Church is the largest church in the City of St. Louis with over forty thousand members. Reverend Graves comments, "I've got to be prepared."

I said, "We'll be broadcasting the opening night event live via the Internet, and JESUS-TV.

They walked passed to alter and up the small stairway that leads to the pulpit. Behind the pulpit is a large baptismal pool and they froze dead in their tracks when they see a body floating face down like a dead fish. Still wearing the bright orange suit from Sunday's church the service is Deacon Murdock floating face down.

Jason runs into the office to call the police, but the office door is locked. The church has a State Of The Art Security System and I can't recall the office ever being locked. Jason rush's back into the sanctuary and tells Shawn, "The office door is locked."

"I was concerned about the security of the ticket, so I locked my office before I left yesterday," responded Shawn to Jason.

I don't like being around dead bodies, especially murdered ones, so I was looking for any reason to get out of there. I believe the other two felt the same way. All three of us leave the baptismal pool area and are walking in the direction of Shawn's office. Shawn nervously fumbles in his pockets for the office keys. Slowly Shawn unlocks the office door and opens the office door. The office looks as through Hurricane Katrina came through, but more torn up. The door to the safe is hanging to one side like it had been blown open with something powerful. Shawn looks into the safe, "I can't believe this!"

"What," I ask but doesn't take a Rocket Scientist to figure it out as Shawn begin pulling clean plastic bags of currency from the safe and laying them on the floor in front of the safe.

I gaze at all those money bags, and I was in the counting room and I know the final total. There is almost $70,000 stacked on the floor in front of the safe. Shawn stands up straight and I bend over and look into the empty safe, and Shawn tells us, "The lottery ticket gone

.

CHAPTER 3

Detective Virginia Breeze

A uniformed police officer is stretching yellow tape across the front entrance of Spirit Temple Pentecostal Christian Church. Two female officers stand along the barricade doing crowd control. Television trucks, vans with attached satellite uplinks, and a News helicopter are flying overhead. The crowd of reporters and onlookers that included members of Spirit Temple Pentecostal Christian Church has gathered along the barricade. Police Squad cars and the Crime Scene Investigator truck slowly drive through the crowd and stops at the barricade. The officers open the barricade and they enter, but as soon as they opened the barricade, a camera operator rushed past the officers with a television camera. An officer ran across the church parking lot and forcibility took the camera from the camera operator and forced him back behind the barricade. The walls are painted from ceiling to floor with various pictures of Christ and a large statue of Christ on one corner, Mary in another, Joseph in another, and the last corner a statue of Michael the Archangel. In the center of the room a large cross with a alter in front. Shawn thought he was alone in the prayer room of Spirit Temple Pentecostal Christian Church Shawn as he prayed, as if he he had any real prayer, "Almighty and merciful God lead and guild me in this time of trouble." Shawn do not notice the strange man at first, he was standing next to Michael the Archangel.

He introduced himself as, "I'm Tony Rome and I've been sent here to help you." Tony extends his hand out to Shawn as he has to look up a a commanding figure of a man that stands every bit of six foot eight, and three hundred pounds as he shook his hand. Tony is a man of means, and even though he was a big man, he looked good in his tailored suit and dress shoes. Still in all, Tony sends out a silent message that he is not one to be messed with. Shawn asks, "Are you with the police?" Without hesitation, Tony replied, "Not exactly." Shawn prides himself for knowing all the members of his church, and Tony Rome was not a member of his church as far as he could remember, and this puzzled Shawn.

Shawn looked at Tony Rome closely, but has no memory of this man, and Shawn asks, "Then if you're not with the police then who are you with?" The door to the prayer room opens and a female with medium complexion and shoulder length black hair, a nice figure enters, and she introduces herself as, "I'm Detective Virginia Breeze and I'm in charge of this investigation." Shawn had intended to introduce Tony Rome, but Tony he was gone.

Detective Breeze looks around the room and does not see anyone other than Shawn, "Something wrong?" Shawn has prayed in that room thousands of times and he knows it like the back of his hand, and there are no windows and there is not but one door and Tony Rome did not go out the door. He could not decide if he was seeing things, or if he had loss his mind. Shawn mind kept returning to the idea of the Knights of the Black Circle

CHAPTER 4

Reverend Shawn Graves

The Graves Estate is tucked away in the rolling hills and meadows outside the city limits of St. Louis. An enormous 12 foot high gate is manned by two armed guards. The long black asphalt, driveway is lined with trees, shrubs, grasses of various varieties like Joe Pye Weed, Ligularia, ironweed, napeta and golden aster. Only a trained eye can determine when the hand of God ends and where the hand of man artistry begins. Shawn and Nichelle Graves own one of the finest luxury estates in St. Louis. Their estate has an attached guest house, and at last appraisal, it valued at a staggering thirty million dollars. The inside is replete with 16 foot ceilings, booked matched marble walls and imported Italian fixtures. The grand hallway connects all the public rooms, making it an ideal location for entertaining. Nichelle is very proud of her home and loves to brag and show it off at any opportunity. She gloats about the sculptural staircase that claims on past forever until you reach the eleven guest bedrooms, gym, and the luxurious master suite. Shawn is a big St. Louis Cardinal fan, and he has been a season ticket holder for five years. His seats are behind home plate. Shawn has never had to pay for his season's tickets, but they come as a gift to the church. The next three Cardinal games are out of town, so he sits on his reclining sofa and watches the game at home from his private screening room.

The Cardinals were playing the Houston Astros in Houston, and Shawn is propped on his reclining sofa. It's the bottom of the fifth ending, and the phone rings. Without much thought or even a glance at the caller ID, Shawn picks up the phone, "Pastor Grave."

"It's Daniel at the front gate, and you need to come out here," says Daniel from the front gate.

"Oh. Why is that?"

Daniel replies in a low voice, "It's Mrs. Murdock, and something's wrong...looks like she's been beat up."

"What! I'm on my way!" Shawn hangs up the phone, and lowers the leg rest of the recliner.

Nichelle comes in carrying the six month old baby, Amber. Shawn is putting on his shoes, "The front gate...It's your mother."

"Daniel just called and said, she been beat up."

Amber starts to car, and their live-in nanny, Thelma comes in and takes Amber from Nichelle's arms and walks up the stairs in the direction of the nursery. Shawn and Nichelle were about to leave when the doorbell rings.

Shawn rushes and opens the door, and Mother Beulah falls forward into Shawn's arms. Shawn and Daniel carry Mother Beulah inside and lay her on the sofa. Daniel asks, "Shall I call 911?"

Mother Beulah starts to come to, "What happened?"

Nichelle tries to hold back the tears, "That's what we would like to know?"

CHAPTER 5

Mother Beulah

YOU'LL NEVER BELIEVE WHAT RAY DID!

I kept telling Nichelle,"I don't want to go to the hospital!" But, Shawn wouldn't hear of it, so he called our family physician, Dr. John Marshall. I could tell from the moment Officer's Jenkins and Kincade walked through the door that there would be more than a few questions and of course the two Paramedics arrive and add to the stress. Shawn has the build of a heavy weight boxer, and Officer Kincade looks at me, and asks, "Who beat you up?"

Officer Jenkins never took his eyes off of Shawn, and as the Paramedic was taking the blood pressure cuff. The Paramedic says, "Wow!"

I asked, "What the reading?"

"168/200…we need to get her to the hospital ASAP," says the Paramedic with a sense of urgency in his voice as his partner loosens the straps with around the gurney.

Officer Jenkins continues glaring at Shawn without blinking, and Officer Kincade restated his question more forcefully, "Who beat you up?"

The Paramedic's rolled the gurney close where I'm sitting, and one of them asked me, "I need for you slide onto the Gurney and we'll get you to Urgent Care."

I don't intend to go to the hospital, but I am not sure how I can avoid it. My solution came through the door with the arrival of my personal physician, Dr. John Marshall and Virginia Breeze.

I looked at one of the Paramedic's identification badge that hung from the side of his belt and it indicates his name as Steve Alton. Everyone in the room knew Dr. Marshall from television. Dr. Marshall is a Chief Medical Editor at the location television station.

I am very surprised, or rather shocked to see Virginia because Virginia is a homicide investigator. As soon as Officer's Kincade and Jenkins seen Virginia they tried to usurp authority, "Detective Breeze? There's no homicide here," commented Officer Jenkins.

Virginia quick tempered response, "You can wait outside...I've got this."

Officer Kincade and Jenkins never moved from the spot they stood, "We'll need to take a report," replied Officer Jenkins.

Virginia said firmly, "That's an order."

From the looks of things, I can tell that Virginia doesn't care for Jenkins and Kincade one iota, so I interject, "Oh Virginia! I'm so glad to see you!"

Nichelle and I watch as the two Officer's step just outside the living room door, but I'm certain they can still hear every word with the door wide open. Nichelle walks over and closes the large solidly built cedar door, so now I know "They can't hear squat now."

Paramedics interrupted and said to Virginia, "We need to rush her to Urgency care right away."

Before Virginia could say anything Dr. Marshall commented,

He looks at Steve and says, "Let me see her chart."

Under the circumstances, Dr. Marshall examined me as best he could, but even he couldn't convince me to go to the emergency room. Nope. Not me. Not today.

"Of course Dr. Marshall," and immediately Steve hands the digital pad he's holding over to Dr. Marshall.

Dr. Marshall asks, "What kind of supplies you have in the unit?"

Steve replies, "Just about anything you need Dr. Marshall."

Dr. Marshall nods and tells Steve, "Let's go take a look?"

Steve informs Dr. Marshall, "No problem. We can administer whatever she needs here."

Dr. Marshall replies, "I like a man that can think fast on his feet," he tells Steve as they walk out the door to the Paramedic unit. Virginia kneels on one knee next to me and asks, "Don't worry I'll take care of everything just tell me what happened."

When you're as famous as my son-in-law Shawn Graves, so any and everything that happens is news. I knew as soon as Daniel called the police the media organizations swarmed the Graves Estate like vultures.

Virginia and her mother, Nadine Dalton have been members of Spirit Temple Pentecostal Christian Church for a long time. When the 9-1-1 call came through it was no accident that Virginia arrived at the Graves Estate. From inside the mansion, I can hear the helicopters flying overhead.

Virginia asked, "Tell us what happened."

Everyone knew Ray Murdock has been seeing other women for years, and everyone knew about Jean Newton. Ray's in his late sixties, and Jean Newton is 32 years old and he's been messing around with her on and off for the past five years.

We used to go to church together, but a year ago Ray said he had some work to do at the office, and told me to drive myself to church and he'd see me at church. Little did I know that I would continue driving myself to church every Sunday from that point on.

I've had the same routine for the past forty years, change clothes and prepare Sunday dinner. When I arrived home, there was a moving truck parked in front of my house, and movers were taking furniture from my house and loading it onto the truck.

I didn't say anything to anyone, but I was thinking, "What's got into Ray?"

"You've wanted to redecorate the house for a long time," commented Nichelle with a smile.

As I was walking up the driveway toward the front door, and another truck pulled up. The truck was from The House of Fresno's.

"That's the place with all the imported and designer furniture," expressed Shawn.

That's the store. The men immediately got out of the truck and I headed into the house. My house was completely empty, and there were men from Ray's construction firm putting up new wall paper and there was new carpeting and drapery. The house was beautiful even if it was empty at that particular moment.

A young man with a goatee walked up to me with a clipboard, and asked "Mrs. Jean Murdock?"

Nichelle shouted, "No way!"

I declared in no uncertain terms, "I'm Mrs. Ray Murdock!"

Mr. Goatee cleaned his throat and looked at his clipboard and started flipped pages, "Oh I see…this order was placed by your daughter, Jean Murdock."

I don't know how I felt, but I told him, "She is not my daughter!"

At about the same time, Jean came down the stairs and looked at Mr. Goatee, "Great! You finally made it!"

Shawn and Nichelle both laugh.

Mr. Goatee recognized Jean immediately, "Ms. Newton…I guess that's Mrs. Murdock now. It's a pleasure to see you again…aha, your maid was about to show me where you wanted the furniture."

It was at that moment I lost all composure and I looked dead at Jean and asked, "What are you doing in my house?"

Ray's construction crew exited the house and went outside, and looked at Jean on the way out and said, "Break time."

Being the socialite she is, she smiled politely and pointed to the living room, "Put everything in there."

Mr. Goatee nodded and left the room, and I smacked Jean so hard that the sound echoed outside, and Jean fell backwards onto the floor yelling, "Help! Help! Why won't someone help me?"

Ray came in, and picked her up off the floor crying, "You assured me that she would not be coming back here!"

Two men from Fresno's came in carrying a brown and gold sofa, and we waited until they brought in everything. I wanted to leave, but something wouldn't let me leave. I thought about it. My father built that house, and I wasn't going to let Jean, Ray, or anyone take my home from me.

Nichelle responded softly, "Okay. We understand that, so what happened next?"

Ray reached in his pocket and gave the man two one hundred dollars bills and said apologetically "I'm sorry for any misunderstanding."

Mr. Goatee inspected the two one hundred dollar bills as if they might be counterfeit, then he said, "No problem. Thank you for shopping at the House of Fresno's."

Ray workers came back into the house and headed upstairs and Jean followed as she tried to wipe blood from her nose. Droplets of blood spotted her pristine white dress. I could hear her talking to one of the workers as she was walking up the stairs, "I just paid six hundred dollars for this dress and now I'll have to throw it away."

The worker told her, "There's more where that came from."

"That true," said Jean.

As soon as everyone was out of sight I looked Ray dead in the eyes, "What do you think you're doing?"

Ray looked at me and grinned, and then that's when he attacked me, and his gorilla hands had a tight grip around my throat, and if his workers hadn't rushed down the stairs to pull him off of me, I'm sure I would be dead now.

Someone and I don't know who, helped me get off the floor and walked me to my car. My purse was still on my arm, and I took my car keys from my purse. Ray ran outside as I was about to get into my car, "You're not taking Jean's car no damn where!"

Ray snatched the keys from my hand, and he started slapping and kicking at me until I left walking down the street. I cried for help, but none came.

Virginia asks, "Didn't the man with you try to help you?"

I replied, "I don't know where he went, but he had disappeared."

Virginia asked, "Did he live in your neighborhood?"

"I'm not sure," I said. Nichelle comes to my house every day and she knows everyone in the neighborhood. As I look around, I don't see Nichelle. I asked, "Where is Nichelle?"

Daniel is standing in the middle of the floor with his hands in his pockets, and he says, "Nichelle left the estate of few minutes ago."

I looked at Shawn, and I can tell by that expression on his face that he knew where Nichelle went.

Dr. Marshall stammered over the words, "I…just gave Nichelle a prescription for Mother Beulah."

I could tell that the Police Officers bought the story. But I've known Virginia since she was little and I don't think she believed it, or if she did she didn't let on. Virginia asked, "Where were you going?"

"Ray keeps all the credit cards in his pocket, so I could go to a hotel, so I was headed to the only other place I could go."

Shawn answered, "Here?"

I tried to hold back the ties as I try to say, "Yes. I continued walking until someone stopped to help me, and it turned out to be the same man that helped me a few minutes earlier.

Shawn looked at Beulah and asked, "Who was he?"

Beulah muttered to herself, "I don't know...Tony something...Tony? Tony Rome!"

The mere mention of the Tony Rome sent Virginia mind back to the good old days of the NSA. She knew Tony's considered a rogue agent, but the one question that keeps twirling around in her mind like a hurricane is:

What's his connection to the church?

CHAPTER 6

Detective Virginia Breeze

THE DAY BEGAN WELL. A fair complexioned young woman, Virginia Breeze is wearing a light pink and white silk robe and walking into the veranda carrying a cup of coffee. The room is maliciously decorated with green Ferns and Spider plants hanging from the ceiling. The patio furniture along with Grandfather clock, complement the veranda with every tick-tock. The six foot tall Candelabra Cactus only adds character to the Sunroom. I hate black coffee. I have to have my cream and sugar, and no I don't eat donuts. It would be pleasant April morning if it weren't pouring down raining. The long hard winter naturally resulted in a decrease in crime, but of course the Ice Storm of 2011 helped keep St. Louis at a virtual standstill. High unemployment and the hot humid weather conditions will set the stage for the Major Case Squad busy season in the City of St. Louis. Experience taught me that most, but not all of the crime will be confined to one region of the city, North St. Louis. The City morgue bubbling over and grabbing for more victims of homicides than Dodge City on its worst day and the funeral services industry will be booming.

A grandmotherly woman with burgundy hair and wearing a pastel dress and brown sandals walks in with a water bucket with a pour spout. The woman doesn't notice Virginia stretched out on the reclining in the lounge chair next to the large cactus. She loving gives each plant a drink of water and speaks as though only she and the plants can communicated with one another, "There you go." She paused and gazes at the plant, "You're welcome." The woman nearly drops and spills the can of water when she spots Virginia sitting in the corner next to the cactus, "Oh my God! You almost scared me to death."

"I'll sorry Mama Nadine," laughs Virginia, "It been a while since I've sat out here…you have a green thumb."

"The plants prefer the humid climate of this room," as she laughs herself. Nadine sits down on the sofa. "I'm surprised you're still here."

The clock tolls six times and Virginia looks at the clock, "I have to go back to Reverend Graves Estate and question Mother Beulah."

Nadine reaches for the television remote and Virginia, "I guess you didn't watch the news last night?"

"I was watching an animated film with Liza and Madison after dinner and then we went bed at about eight thirty," states Nadine. "Why what's going on?" she asks.

I decided it would be better to hear it from me than one of the ladies from the church, "Reverend Graves found Deacon Murdock dead last night."

Nadine brings her palms together like she is about to pray, then cries out, "Say what?"

"He was found dead in the baptismal pool yesterday morning."

Nadine leans back on the sofa, "I've never liked that thing...they call it a baptismal pool, but that's an indoor summing pool."

Nadine has been member of Spirit Temple Pentecostal Christian Church since the 1950's, but I became a member about a year before my husband Nicholas and I were married. Even though I had been baptized in the Catholic Church, the former pastor, John Graves insisted that I be baptized, but that was at the old church not the new one. I commented to Nadine, "Yeah, I never noticed that until yesterday."

"Oh well. With your job you don't spend as much time at church as I do," she comments, "I'd better check on Beulah and see how she's doing," mentioned Nadine.

Virginia glanced at the Grandfather clock, "A quarter after six, and I have a long drive to the Graves Estate."

Nadine looks at Virginia strangely, "What do you need to question Beulah for?"

As soon as I leave I know those church woman will start calling my house and running their mouths, and since I'd already told Nadine part of the story I may as well tell her the rest of the story. "Deacon Murdock beat Beulah up last night.

Nadine lowers her head, "I don't know why someone would stay with someone so abusive all those years."

I choose not to comment because I really had no idea that had been going on, or why the church would allow him to continue as deacon of the church. I would have booted him out on his head a long time ago.

Virginia is stuck in a traffic jam on Interstate 270. 270 is one of those highways where you can fly at seventy miles an hour and still be bumper to bumper. There have been times I have driven almost ninety miles an hour without blinking, but this is not one of those days. I am already later than I intended, but that does not really matter that much. I have a lot of flexibility to come and go as it suits me. When I think about it…I'm not sure why the St. Louis Police Department hired me, but maybe someone gave him no other choice. When I say him, I am referring to Captain Cornelius West. I can only speak well of Captain West. He has been honest his entire life, and can be counted among the most honorable of people and I hope he remains what he is.

Virginia pulls into the far left and signals her turn at the next exit. She breaks her speed to thirty miles an hour, and comes to a complete stop at the traffic light. "Shit…I hate this light…it holds to long." I glance at the convenience store across the street, and it's jammed packed with gas at $3.19 a gallon. Turning on the radio. I love my R&B music, but I like listening to the Lucius Dyamond show. Lucius is a local DJ that dabbles with playwriting. I think it's just a clever way to avoid paying taxes on a surplus income. All of his plays are performed in churches and everyone pays cash at the door. It is the perfect setup. Turning up the volume, "This is Lucius Dyamond! Check those lottery tickets from Saturday night's drawing! There's a winner and it was purchased here in St. Louis! I checked mine, and I don't have a Billion Dollar lottery ticket!"

Virginia says, "Jesus." The light finally changes to green as Virginia car continues straight down a private road. She passes a police patrol car parked along the side of the road. My guess he already ran my plates, and knows I am a cop that is way outside my jurisdiction. I am less than a half a mile away from the Graves Estate's main gate, but I must have spoken to soon. I looked out my rearview mirror, and flashing close behind me the Police Patrol car.

My philosophy, "Better to be safe than sorry," so without much thought I pull my Kimber CDP II .45 that I keep concealed in a special holster under the edge of the driver's seat. It's just small enough to tuck under my thigh and not be noticed. As I glance out my left rearview mirror...I can't believe my eyes. It was none other than Christian Kane.

Reaching and turning down the radio. Christian is six foot four and two hundred twenty pounds with pale white skin. Even if you had no idea that Christian is NSA...his expensive shoes would make anyone suspicious. Christian walks over to the passenger side of Virginia car and gets in, and she asks, "What are you doing here?"

Christian's sly grin told me more than I needed to know, and I don't have any idea why he's masquerading as a common police officer. "You've been reactivated."

Shake my head in disbelief I asks, "Why?"

"There has been a rash of good fortune among the parishioners of Spirit Temple Pentecostal Christian Church," says Christian in a dead serious tone.

"What do you mean? Good Fortune?" I ask.

Christian reaches into his pocket and hands me a small computer storage device, "The details are on the device."

I looked at the device. It made of gold and it seems to be a bit more sophisticated than what I'm used to seeing, "Alright."

"A large number of people from the same church have been having a run of good luck playing the lottery," and "Looks like Ray Murdock's luck just ran out."

"You mean to tell murder investigation is tied to defrauding the lottery," states Virginia.

Christian looks at me, "Someone has figured out our lottery gaming system, and have hit the State's Fantasy 7 game seventeen times for over fifty million dollars."

I laugh, "I go to that church, and the majority of the people don't have the ability or education to be capable of something at this level." I knew full well with a church that large that just about anything was possible.

Christian opens the door to get out, but stops and turns to Virginia. "I know it goes against your grain, but we need this one by the book."

"You know I always go by the book."

"Yeah, but try not to leave a bunch of dead bodies in the process," he said sarcastically.

I smile at Christian, "I always go back the book."

"It's the stuff that's not in the book that leaves a bloody trail behind you," comments Christian "An old fashioned investigation is the only way to get at the bottom of what's going on."

I ask, "Why me?"

Gesturing with his right hand, "They already know and trust you, and that's worth its weight in gold."

"Who do you think I am? Jessica Fletcher?" He gets out and slams the car door and walks back to his police car, and pulls a U-Turn and hits Interstate-270 and disappears out of sight.

CHAPTER 7

Mother Beulah Murdock

THIS IS NO EXACGERATION, but Virginia sat and listened to Mother Beulah entire story, and everyone was waiting for something, but what? Virginia laid her cell phone on the coffee table in front of Mother Beulah, "

From the moment Virginia walks into the Feng Shui Room I could tell she was surprised to see Christians into this Asian Mysticism and I would never admit to it, but it was Nichelle and that decorator. I think her name was Ching Sue Ye. I believe Shawn would have been fine with just pictures of Jesus, but that's my opinion. After all I never had to live here, not until now.

Virginia in her normal take charge style, "I'll need to record your statement for the record."

I was surprised and shocked, "Shawn!"

Shawn in his best calming, reassuring manner, "It will be okay…it's just procedure."

Virginia looks at my two black eyes and fat lip, "Oh my God!"

I fail at attempting to reassure Virginia, "I'm fine…The doctor got me fixed up last night."

"You didn't look this bad last night," observed Virginia, "Looks as though you've been in boxing match since I last seen you." I tried to make myself look better as best I could by covering the bruises with makeup and wearing a wig I keep here but Nichelle said, "You look like you used a putty knife to apply your makeup."

Virginia looks at Shawn and Nichelle carefully before she requests, "I need to question Mother Beulah in private."

I'd never been in trouble in my life, but I feel like things are coming together to be trouble, "I asks them to be here, or I do I need to call my attorney?"

Virginia replied, "That won't be necessary...I just wanted to ask a couple of questions and get a little bit more information about you and Deacon Murdock's separation."

I've known Virginia from since she was a small child, and I could tell by the glare in her eyes there was something more on her mind, but I decided to play the waiting game. "Everyone knew Ray Murdock has been seeing other women for years and everyone knew about Jean Newton."

Nichelle jumps in, "Ray's in his late sixties, and Jean Newton is 32 years old and he's been messing around with her on and off for the past five years."

"We used to go to church together, but a year ago Ray said he had some work to do at the office, and told me to drive myself to church and he'd see me at church. Little did I know that I would continue driving myself to church every Sunday from that point on."

"Mom's had the same routine for the past forty years, change clothes and prepare Sunday dinner," comments Nichelle.

"Yes. When I arrived home, there was a moving truck parked in front of my house, and movers were taking furniture from my house and loading it onto the truck." Mother Beulah pauses for a moment to catch her breath, "I didn't say anything to anyone, but I was thinking, what's got into Ray?"

"You've wanted to redecorate the house for a long time," commented Nichelle with a smile.

"As I was walking up the driveway toward the front door, and another truck pulled up. The truck was from The House of Fresno's."

"That's the place with all the imported and designer furniture," expressed Shawn.

"That's the store." Beualah continues, "The men immediately got out of the truck and I headed into the house. My house was completely empty, and there were men from Ray's construction firm putting up new wall paper and there was new carpeting and drapery. The house was beautiful even if it was empty at that particular moment," shaking her head.

Inquisitively Virginia wanted to know, "While you were at Church?"

"Well yeah. Between Sunday School, and Church they crew had a seven hour jump, and being they are professional commercial contractors makes it all the difference in the world." I tried explaining to Virginia. "A young man with a goatee walked up to me with a clipboard, and asked "Mrs. Jean Murdock?"

Nichelle shouted, "No way!"

I declared in no uncertain terms, "I'm Mrs. Ray Murdock!"

"Mr. Goatee cleaned his throat and looked at his clipboard and started flipped pages, Oh I see…this order was placed by your daughter, Jean Murdock."

"I don't know how I felt, but I told him," "She is not my daughter!"

"At about the same time, Jean came down the stairs and looked at Mr. Goatee, and said, Great! You finally made it!"

Shawn sat on Beulah's right and Nichelle to the left on the sofa, and Virginia sat in a strange looking chair that looks and feels like a cold wet sponge. Virginia tried adjusting herself with little success, so she got up and walks over to the coffee table and picks up the cell phone and glances at the recording display, then lays it back down in front of Beulah. Virginia is not the type to sit in a lower chair, so he squatted down on the floor in front of the coffee table. Virginia quietly instructs Mother Beulah, "Please continue."

"Mr. Goatee recognized Jean immediately, "Ms. Newton…I guess that's Mrs. Murdock now." It's a pleasure to see you again…your maid was about to show me where you wanted the furniture."

"It was at that moment I lost all composure and I looked dead at Jean and yelled," "What are you doing in my house?" "Ray's construction crew exited the house and went outside, and looked at Jean on the way out and said," "Break time."

Nichelle jumps in again, "Being the socialite she is, she smiled politely."

I am trying to continue and get this over with, "Jean pointed to the living room, "Put everything in there." "Mr. Goatee nodded and left the room, and I smacked Jean so hard that the sound echoed outside." "And Jean fell backwards onto the floor yelling," "Help! Help! Why won't someone help me?"

Anyone can look at me and tell I've never missed a meal, and I must admit, "I put my entire two hundred and thirty pounds into that lick. I only wished I would have used my fist!"

Virginia smiles, "I bet you wanted to kill her?"

"You bet I did! I just wasn't sure how."

Shawn, "Mother be careful what you say on tape."

Nichelle was looking at the phone like she wanted to take it and smash it against the wall, but Virginia picked up the phone and held it in one hand closer to Mother Beulah.

"Ray came in, and picked her up off the floor crying" "She said to Ray," "You assured me that she would not be coming back here!"

"Two men from Fresno's came in carrying a brown and gold sofa, and we waited until they brought in everything. I wanted to leave, but something wouldn't let me leave. I thought about it. My father built that house, and I wasn't going to let Jean, Ray, or anyone take my home from me."

Nichelle responded softly, "Okay. We understand that, so what happened next?"

"Ray reached in his pocket and gave the man two one hundred dollars bills and said apologetically" "I'm sorry for any misunderstanding."

"Mr. Goatee inspected the two one hundred dollar bills as if they might be counterfeit or something," "Then he said, "No problem. Thank you for shopping at the House of Fresno's."

"Ray workers came back into the house and headed upstairs and Jean followed as she tried to wipe blood from her nose. Droplets of blood spotted her pristine white dress. I could hear her talking to one of the workers as she was walking up the stairs, "I just paid six hundred dollars for this dress and now I'll have to throw it away."

"The worker told her," "There's more where that came from."

"That true, said Jean."

"As soon as everyone was out of sight I looked Ray dead in the eyes, "What do you think you're doing?"

"Ray looked at me and grinned, and then that's when he attacked me, and his gorilla hands had a tight grip around my throat with one hand and punching me with another."

Nichelle comments, "If his workers hadn't rushed down the stairs to pull Ray off of Mom... I'm sure she would be dead now."

In cheap attempt to bait someone, anyone in the room Virginia says, "But Deacon Murdock's the one that's dead?"

Nichelle commanded Shawn, "Honey get our attorney out here!"

Shawn get up, "Excuse me," and he leaves the room.

I love this mansion, but I don't care for the location. It takes forever to get out here from downtown St. Louis. By the time the lawyer makes the drive Virginia will be gone. I tried to gather my thoughts are not be to distracted, "Someone and I don't know who, helped me get off the floor. He walked me to my car. My purse was still on my arm, and I took my car keys from my purse. Ray ran outside as I was about to get into my car," Ray yells, "You're not taking that car no damn where!"

Ray snatched the keys from my hand, and he started slapping and kicking at me until I left walking down the street. I cried for help, but none came.

Virginia wanted to know, "What about the construction crew?"

"Well you know how that works. I looked up at the upstairs windows and Jean and the workers were watching, but they did nothing."

Hostilely Nichelle says, "If they want their job...they'd better not say or do anything!"

I tell them, "The workers don't mess with Ray!"

Virginia looks at Nichelle, "Is Ray Murdock your father?"

"Yes, but he does not allow me to call him Dad."

Virginia asks, "Didn't you think that was strange?"

I was about to answer, but before I had a chance Nichelle stopped me, and informed Virginia, "It was done for business purposes."

Virginia looked Puzzled, "Business?"

I know Nichelle bought the act, but I didn't I know that Virginia is smart. Nichelle answers, "Yes I'm Vice President and Co-owner of Murdock construction."

Looking around the room, there was no sign of Shawn anywhere, and I could tell that Virginia was going to be to inquisitive, so I tried to continue where I left off, "I continued walking until someone stopped to help me, and it turned out to be the same man that helped me off the floor a few minutes earlier."

Virginia asks, "Who was he?"

Beulah muttered to herself, "I don't know…Tony something…Tony. Tony Rome!"

Out of the blue, Virginia's tone changes, "A few of your members have been a little lucky lately, and I want to know what you know about the lottery."

I froze, but Nichelle quickly replies, "Gambling is a sin."

"I didn't ask about the bible and gambling. I want to know why there are so many lottery winner's coming out of Spirit Temple Pentecostal Christian Church?"

Neither I nor Nichelle said another word after Shawn returned to the room. Shawn informed Virginia, "Our Attorney will be contacting you Detective Breeze as soon as he gets out of court." Shawn remains standing and ready to show Virginia out.

The Eleventh Commandment: Thou shalt not get caught lying.

CHAPTER 8

Mother Beulah Murdock

I'M NOT AFRAID TO SAY IT, "I'm glad that bastard's dead and hope he rots in peace."

Nichelle asks, "Mom what's the matter with you?"

"Just because I have sense enough not to mourn his passing doesn't mean anything's wrong with me," replies Mother Beulah.

As Nichelle and Mother Beulah are getting into Nichelle's BMW, Nichelle asks, "Don't you think it's important that you appear to be the grieving widow?"

"I didn't kill him and I don't know who did, but I'm not going to pretend a lie," comments Mother Beulah to her daughter, Nichelle as she stops at the Graves Estate's Main gate. Nichelle flashes a smile and waves at the guard Daniel.

"Why so friendly with the hired help?"

"I don't know what you're talking about," snaps Nichelle.

"You never smile and wave like that at your husband," observes Mother Beulah, "He's not even a member of our church. How in the world did he get a job working for you and Shawn?"

"I'm not sure, but I think he's someone Shawn and Ray met through the prison ministry."

"He's a convicted felon, and he's carrying a gun!"

Nichelle started fumbling with the radio, "You know…Uh?"

I know Nichelle's is stumbling over some lie, "Uh-nothing"

"I was going to say Shawn knows people, and a license to carry a gun was no big deal."

Nichelle pulls into the driveway of the Murdock Estate and parks her BMW behind a brand new black Cadillac. It was sitting in the driveway, and Nichelle stops her car behind it and she and Mother Beulah get out "Now I've heard it all. I'll wipe after that load of crap."

I looked at my car as we walk to the door. Nichelle tries her keys to get into the house, and they still work. The first thing most people do is change the locks on the doors, but not Ray Murdock, the old keys still fit the doors. In my opinion, Ray and Jean should have gotten their own house. It's not like Ray was poor or anything. "My mind is made up and Jean's getting a hunk of it, plus I'm throwing her out of my house."

Nichelle looks back at her mother's car and I explain to Nichelle, "After today, you're finished driving me around."

"You'll be okay," trying to console her mother.

"My father bought this land and built the original house so we would always have a home, and I'll be damn if I let anyone take it!"

Nichelle says, "I don't feel right about coming in like this. I think we should go to our lawyer or the police." Nichelle hears conversation and hammering, and looks around before going inside the house, and notice two men working on the roof of the mansion next door. The men have stopped working decide to sit and watch Nichelle and Mother Beulah as they enter the house.

Nichelle comments, "I would have changed the locks a long time ago."

Nichelle follows Mother Beulah in, but she deliberately "leaves the door open.

Mother Beulah yells at Nichelle, "Close my front door!"

36

Nichelle slams the door, "Wow! This house is beautiful, and to think he done all this for Jean Newton. They walk into the living room and the walls are painted orange along one wall and wall paper along another wall. The furniture was some crazy brown and orange design. Even the kitchen has been totally remodeled with brand is new appliances including a dishwasher and brand new cabinets. The kitchen looks as though it never gets used.

Sitting her purse on the kitchen counter, "No one can grasp what Ray sees in a woman that does not have any skill for doing anything."

Nichelle keeps looking around, "The house is clean because Ray hired someone from the church to come in and do the cleaning."

"I've been talking about it for years, but Ray refused."

Nichelle laughs, "When people found out, and I don't know who done it, but they slashed all four of the tires of his truck."

"It was after the tire slashing that he hired Lashonda Newton to come in and do the cleaning."

While Nichelle is looking through all the kitchen cabinets and laughing, "There is no food in this house."

I started opening closing cabinets and drawers, and they were all empty, "If I didn't know any better I'd swear they were getting the house ready to be sold."

Nichelle tells her Mother, "I told Ray that he should not allow Lashonda, but he refused to listen."

"I didn't know it then, but I think it was about Jean the entire time."

Nichelle paused to open the refrigerator door, "Well look at this!"

Just one look into the empty and cold refrigerator, "Jean likes to eat at fancy restaurants all the time."

Ray told me,"Lashonda should have an opportunity to redeem herself," replies Mother Beulah.

Nichelle stood there with the refrigerator door open and looks at her mother, "Redeemed from what?"

"I told Ray...let Jesus handle the redemption, but not in my house."

Nichelle, "I can't believe Jean hasn't heard us in the house." "That does seem strange, but she's strange."

There is a sound of someone at the door. Nichelle panics and whispers, "I knew this was a bad idea," and shuts the refrigerator door. The deadbolt unlocks with a thud and the front door opens.

Lashonda comes in. Lashonda and her bad weave with clothes to match along with her tabletop butt that seems to go on and on. Lashonda walks in carrying grocery bags and, "I thought that looked like your car Nichelle." Lashonda sits her bags on the kitchen counter next to Mother Beulah purse then looks at Nichelle and Mother Beulah states, "Beulah you shouldn't be here."

Nichelle looks at Lashonda, "Since when have you been on the first name basis with Mother Beulah Murdock?"

With a quick roll of her neck and eyes Lashonda fires back, "I am not going call her Mother anything, Sister anything or Mrs. anything. She is not anything!"

Mother Beulah eyes tears, then turn fire engine red and Nichelle raises her voice, "You're the most disrespectful Gutter Witch I've ever came in contact with."

Mother Beulah looks at Lashonda and says to Lashonda while pointing at the front door, "This is my house and you are fired!" "Now get out!"

Lashonda puts her hands on her hips in defiance, "I don't work for either of you and this is not your house!"

I grabbed Lashonda by the hair and attempt to snatch her brains out, but all I had was a hand full of mildewed hair, "When was the last time you washed that filthy head!"

Nichelle stood laughing while struggling to pull her mother off of Lashonda. Beulah releases her grip on Lashonda head after she bites Mother Beulah on the forearm, and she yells, "Ouch!"

Mother Beulah cradles her arm to stop the bleeding, "I hope you don't have some disease."

Nichelle pulls a white handkerchief from the pocket of her jacket and puts it over the bite mark, and looks in Lashonda direction and says, "Mom I hope the hospital does not require you to get rabies shot!?

Lashonda gets angry puts up her fist and starts bobbing and weaving like a boxer, "You two think you're bad!"

Mother Beulah, "Jesus!"

Lashonda remarks, "He's not here today!" She Lashonda takes a swing, but and socks Nichelle square in the nose.

Tray walks in and yells, "What in hell going on in here?" He grabs Lashonda and tells her, "Go upstairs and get your Aunt Jean and I'll take care of this!"

Lashonda walks toward the stairs as Nichelle is nursing a bloody nose, "Shawn's not going to like any of this."

Looking Tray dead in the face, "This is my house and I want all of you out!"

Tray laughs hysterically, "You dumb bitch. You need to check the deed...Ray had Uncle Perry changed it to a Deed of Survivorship and as of last night, this house became Jean's!"

The Sirens are deafening, the police bang on the front door. Lashonda runs down the stairs in tears, and for points to Mother Beulah, "Aunt Jean is dead!"

Nichelle, Beulah and Tray response in perfect harmony, "WHAT?"

The police burst through the door with their weapons drawn and "Freeze!"

Tray, Nichelle and Lashona raise their hands.

I continue holding my bloody arm, and the Officer looks and Mother Beulah and yells, "I said, GET YOUR HANDS UP!" I dropped the bloody handkerchief onto the floor.

Nichelle says, "I'm the wife of Pastor Shawn Graves and this is my mother!"

Lashonda shouts, "Nobody cares whose wife you are!"

The Officer looks at the blood on the front of Nichelle purple and white blouse and Lashonda torn out hair on the kitchen floor, Lashonda cries and points directly at Mother Beulah and Nichelle, "They broke in and killed Aunt Jean!" In an act that even top A-List Ocar winners would have problems out preforming Lashonda next move topped it off. Only a good liar can collapses in fits of blubbing and anguish onto the floor.

I should have listened to Nichelle and allowed her to contact her lawyer, but now it's too late. Virginia Breeze enters the house and looks at everything and everyone around her and in a stern voice, "Cuff them."

The Officer takes Mother Beulah and Nichelle outside. A few minutes later another Officer comes out carrying Mother Beulah's purse out and opens it on the hood of the patrol car and out falls a gun and several credit cards with the name of Jean Newton on them. People are on the sidewalks in front of their homes watching.

Mother Beulah cries out as she looks at the gun and credit cards, "What's going on?" "I've never owned any guns."

The Officer starts reading Mother Beulah and Nichelle their rights as people from the neighborhood gather around. One of the men yells, "Why are you arresting Mother Beulah Mudock and Nichelle Graves?"

Lashonda comes outside shouting, "She broke into my house"

Another yells to the police, "I know you don't believe that little tramp!"

Tray puts his arm around Lashonda, and walks her to the Cadillac and unlocks the door and helps Lashonda into the car. A man yells, "Where do think you're going in Mother Beulah's car?"

A crowd gathers around and refuses to allow Tray to back out of the driveway. An officer walks over to the car and asks, "Whose car is this?"

Tray reaches over, opens the glove compartment, pulls out some papers, and hands them to the Officer. It is the title and registration and lists the name of Lashonda Newton on it. Tray goes on to explain that, "Mr. Ray Murdock sold the car to Lashonda because Aunt Jean never learned to drive, and Beulah Murdock was too old and feeble minded to drive."

The Officer looks over the papers, then hands them back to Tray and orders the crowd, "Back away from the car!"

A van pulls up in front of the Murdock Mansion, and in the middle of the street, and Police in full riot gear begin jumping out, and a strong male voice announced on a loud speaker, "Return to your homes!"

Tray backs out of the driveway, and as he drives off the crowd shout profanities at Lashonda and Tray as they slowly drive pass the crowd. One of the men, Stephen Emerson looks at his thirteen-year-old son, Mike and tells him, "Go into the house and call Reverend Graves at the church and let him know what's going on.

CHAPTER 9

Dr. Benjamin Hussein

My appearance is everything and being of Middle Eastern decent many people think I am a foreigner even though I was born in the United States. My name is Dr. Benjamin Hussein. I am less than happy with this black pen stripped suit with a white shirt with a light blue fat tie, the jacket of the suit sleeves are too big at the cuff and a too long at the sleeves. I will be speaking to my tailor because this is not my suit.

Dr. Ahmed Bhat is completing his final year residency and he will be a full Medical Examiner. Ahmed walks in carrying a stack of printed reports and lays them down on Dr. Hussein's desk, "These are the toxicology results for Raymond Murdock," says Ahmed.

Looking carefully over the results, "This is interesting," responds Dr. Hussein.

Ahmed, "Macy said you could call her if you had any questions."

Flipping through the pages, "Ah...I don't think it's Macy I need to consult."

"She told me she contacted Doctor Dana Khan."

I tried to keep my composure, but without any thought I snapped at Ahmed, "She should have consulted me first!"

"That's my fault...I authorized that samples to be flown to Dr. Khan's lab for further analysis yesterday...Dr. Khan should already have them."

Yelling at Ahmed, "Did you even consider the cost of consulting a Nobel Prize Winning Botanist?"

Ahmed eyes widened, but he said nothing.

I demanded to know, "Well did you!"

"Cost was the last thought on my mind, but rather…" I interrupted Ahmed.

"I don't want to hear your lame excuses!"

Ahmed puzzled, "Should I prepare the body for a complete autopsy?"

Continuing to look over the crime scene toxicology reports, "Prepare for an external autopsy," says Dr. Hussein as he looks over a release form for Friendly Spirit Mortuary.

"We should open him up just for procedural purposes?" asks Ahmed.

"No need to…It's obvious the cause of death was drowning, but it seems he was doomed to die even had he not drowned!"

"But we still should do a autopsy and cover all out bases," presses Ahmed.

Dr. Hussein, "I need to contact Detective Breeze!"

"Due to toxicology results, I think there should be a full autopsy completed on the body," asserts Ahmed.

In a sarcastic tone, Dr. Hussein gets up from his desk and straightens his tie and signs the release forms, "That's why I'm the Chief Medical Examiner and you're not!"

Ahmed walks out of Dr. Hussein's office mumbling, "This is not right."

Virginia has arrives fully rested and juiced up on caffeine. Ahmed escorts Virginia to the Chief Medical Examiner's Office.

I could her thud of her boots before she arrived at my door. I know Detective Breeze from reputation, and if there was going to be a problem it was going to come from Virginia Breeze. I hate female law enforcement officers. Thank goodness their not men, but they are not quite women either, but something closer to a wild animal. Ahmed knocks before opening the door and he and Detective enter.

Virginia hates being kept waiting, but I could care less, so I hesitate before looking up at Detective Breeze, and opening a file labelled Raymond Murdock."The preliminary results indicate that cause of death is drowning, but he was going to die eventually anyway."

"What do you mean?" asked Virginia.

"The general consensus is drowning, but he still would have died from being poisoned."

Virginia asks, "What kind of poison?"

Doctor Hussein says, "That's what so baffling...Poison Control's even stumped."

Virginia interjects, "I would've thought the Federal Database would list all known poisons?"

Gathering his words, "Ordinarily yes, but in this case this particular poison is not common or known, but I'm going to consult Doctor Dana Khan."

"The name does not sound familiar," says Virginia as she takes a small notepad and pen from her pocket, and writes down the name, Doctor Dana Khan.

"Doctor Khan is a Botanist at the Saad research facility in in Los Angeles."

"So you think the poison is organic?"

Dr. Hussein smiles at Virginia's intelligence, "The plant is of unknown origin?"

"Let me get this straight, I'm looking for a plant of some kind?" inquires Virginia.

"I felt it necessary to get an expert involved, so I contacted Doctor Khan."

Ahmed glares at Doctor Hussein with complete contempt, and walks out without saying a word.

I could tell Virginia detected a problem between Ahmed and me, and she said, "What's wrong with the good doctor?"

I attempt to laugh it off with a snigger, "He's not yet a doctor, but he's well on his way." I could tell the way she looked back in Ahmed's direction that she didn't believe one word of it.

Virginia asks, "Is this all you know about the plant."

I thought for a moment before answering her, "It has some abnormal properties and characteristics.

She asked, "The plant would not be native to North America, and it would require special conditions to grow?"

She continued taking short-hand notes of my every word, so I handed her a copy of the file and tell her, "Absolutely and when I know more I will let you know."

When will the body be released?" asked Virginia.

I stood up to show Detective Breeze to the door, "This afternoon."

Ahmed heard the sound and her boots as she walked down the hall. Ahmed was about to follow Virginia, but I called out to him, "Where do you think you're going?"

Ahmed and Virginia both stopped and looked back at me, and Ahmed replies, "To escort Detective Breeze out."

I continue watching as Ahmed and Virginia walk to the end of the corridor, then disappear around the corner.

CHAPTER 10

Dr. Ahmed Bhat

Dr. Ahmed Bhat and Virginia walk down another long corridor, and she notices, "If I didn't know any better, I'd swear we were taking a different way out?"

I answer her, "Sort of?"

"What was that all about in Doctor Hussein office?

As pleasantly as possible, "We had a difference of opinion regarding a certain procedure"

"It got a little tense for a moment."

"I'm sure you're heard a lot of stories about this place and how things work."

In her typical straight to the point style, "What are you getting at?"

"I felt that a complete external autopsy should have been completed, but he didn't."

She stopped dead in her tracks, and looked dead at me, "What?"

At once I knew I'd opened a can of worms, "Normally with a straight drowning an external autopsy would not be needed, but since this involved a lethal dose of an unknown substance, then an external autopsy is always done."

"I can't believe this," exclaimed Virginia.

"I contacted Doctor Khan yesterday without Dr. Hussein knowledge and I had biological sample flown to Doctor Khan Laboratory."

They continue walking down the hall until they come to a large set of double doors, and Ahmed passes his security card over the square grey pad and the doors open.

Virginia finished my sentence, "When he found out he got angry?"

I looked around at all the closed office doors, "Doctor Khan is not just a botanist, but she is also specializes in Forensic Pathology." I reach into my lab coat pocket and pull Doctor Khan's card from my pocket and give it to Detective Breeze. "If you get her out here, she can do a complete autopsy, but she will have to do it before Ray Murdock is embalmed."

I shook her hand, "Good luck Detective Breeze."

"Thank you Doctor Bhat, and I'll be in touch."

I watched through the glass doors as she got into her car and left. I felt a sense of relief as I walked down the long corridor passed the closed door, but the last door I came to was standing open, and a man standing there. I looked at the odd looking man. He seemed a little overdressed for this type of office, and I knew instantly, "You shouldn't be in here."

Nervously, "I'm sorry...I was looking for the office of Doctor Hussein."

I pointed him in the direction of Doctor Hussein office and he walked in the direction of the Doctor Hussein's office as I reached to close the door, someone in a ski-mask grabbed me from behind and shoved me into the office and slammed the door shut.

He reached into his pocket and pulled a gun from the inside of his jacket, and while he pointed the weapon at me, "Don't move." He reaches into his left pocket and pulled a round circular object out, and begins locking it onto the end of the gun. I ran to the door, but the door was locked from the outside. I looked around the white cold room and realized where I was, the locker room where the bodies are kept before pickup, "Who are you?"

The man pulls out one of the drawers, and says, "That's not important."

"You're not going to get with this," I told him as I climbed into the locker.

His only reply, "I already have."

I demand, "What do you want?"

I squeeze my eyes close as hard as I can as he points the gun at my skull, "Your dead!"

The man opens fire and Ahmed collapses and dies and the steel table.

He slams the door close with Ahmed inside, and leaves.

CHAPTER 11

Detective Virginia Breeze

Detective, Virginia Breeze is at her desk looking through crime scene photos from Spirit Temple Pentecostal Christian Church. She sits in a closed office cubicle flipping from one photograph to the next. First is the shot of Ray Murdock floating face down in the baptismal pool followed another snapshot of Shawn's office with the door to the safe hanging by a single hinge. Virginia thinks to herself, "There something more going on."

A hefty man in his mid-fifties with sandy grey hair enters Virginia's cubicle without as much as a polite knock at the door, Captain Cornelius West is his name. Each strandstrand of hair he has left on top of his head remains fiercely loyal unto the end and stands at attention awaiting orders from the commander on top of his balding head. He slams the door behind himself and sits down in the computer chair with wheels on the side of Virginia's desk, "What do you think?"

"Jeez, I think the murder was looking for something in the safe, but what I can't be certain."

"They had to be. After all who breaks into a safe and leaves ten thousand dollars cash untouched?"

"Have you spoken to the Medical Examiner yet?"

Cornelius goes into the next cubical and grabs a chair and rolls it next to Virginia and sits down. "I was at Doctor Hussein's office about an hour ago, and I need a warrant hold the remains of Ray Murdock."

"You need a what?"

"I need a warrant to hold Ray Murdock's body until the Forensic Pathologist arrives."

Captain West leans forward in chair, "That kind of warrant does not grow on a tree!"

"Take a look at this," and I hand the autopsy results file to Captain West, and he begins looking at the blank sketch of the man before he begins flipping through the pages to the toxicology results then he closes the file and lays it on her desk.

"I may have trouble getting a warrant for this," replies Captain West.

I picked up the folder and turned to the last page, "Read the last paragraph, and you'll see why I need the warrant."

Cornelius slowly reads the last paragraph, "Poison!" He flips

the front page and looks of the blank sketch, "I don't get it? Did he or didn't Doctor Hussein do an autopsy?"

I leaned back in my chair, "According to Doctor Hussein's Intern, Doctor Ahmed Bhat, Doctor Hussein did an external autopsy."

"In all my years, I've never heard of such a thing," retorts Captain West as he stands up, "All right. I'll see what I can do."

Captain West opens the cubicle door, and I knowing Captain West as long as I have, he has two speeds, slow and slower, "I need the full autopsy done before the Undertaker embalms the body, or all bets are off."

Captain West scratches his beard as he turns to leave, "Yeah, I've got you covered." Denisha Logan.

Looking down at the stack of crime scene photographs and picking up the first photograph on top, the colourful print of the door of the safe hanging from a single hinge. Absorbed in the print and various theories and images danced in her mind, but it's a loud knocking at the door broke her concentration, "Come in!"

Jack Mangano, Chief of the bomb squad enters carry a folder in his large hands. He is six feet and seven inches tall, wearing white and grey military fatigues and combat boots. At two hundred fifty pounds, only a fool would attempt to fight him hand to hand. He's not a friendly type, but can be suspicious of his surroundings, "Hello. I need to talk to you about one of your cases."

"Sure come on in," and she lays down the photograph as Jack walks up behind her and with the advantage of his height, he has a clear line of sight as he looks at the photograph.

"That's what I need to discuss with you," he picks up the photograph and sits down in the computer chair next to Virginia desk.

"I was just looking at the crime scene photographs."

Jack lays the photograph to the side of the desk and opens the folder he's carrying, "That a vault."

I picked up the photograph and looked at it again, "That kind of vault is not for sale to the general public, but sold mainly banks and armour car companies."

Jack takes the image and lays it down in front of Virginia and points to the brand name embossed in gold in the front on the outer edge of the safe, "Do you see? Fogarty. Fogarty only makes and sells these type of small vaults to banks and armour car companies."

I continue looking at the photo and inquired of Jack, "Aren't bank vaults supposed to be impossible to break into?"

"By ordinary means, yes and when I say ordinary means, I'm referring to a crowbar or something like that," Jack explained.

I continue looking at the photograph, "Interesting. Well someone managed to figure out a weakness in the safe."

Jack tells me, "It took experience, and the only types of people with experience with explosive are military and construction companies that specialize in demolition,"

I say, "Huh, demolition?"

Jack's eyes widen, "Like the kind Ray Murdock's company specializes in."

I can tell by Jack expression there was some other detail, but I beat him to the punch, "Murdock Construction?"

All of a sudden, a question enters my minds ear drum, "Had it been explosives wouldn't it have made a tremendous noise?"

Jack describes what he means with a series and hand and finger gestures, "Not all explosives have sound, and some explosives can be placed at a central point such as a door, and with a small boom…take off the entire door."

I looked at the photograph again, "They left $10,000 in cash. Whatever was worth all the trouble was worth more than the cash?"

Jack failed in his endeavours to adopt a smile, "And it was well worth the effort to kill someone in order to take possession of it."

I examined the photograph again, "Indeed it was, but what was it?

CHAPTER 12

Detective Virginia Breeze

Captain West chooses do his weekly tag along and with me and today of all days. It's a quarter till twelve and traffic is moving like icy Sorghum Molasses. If I'd been alone I would have used the sirens to get through traffic, but today is not the day. Captain West comments, "Your report indicated you'd already spoken to Dr. Hussein."

I answer in a short agitated tone, "I going to see Dr. Bhat." I don't like partners, and sidekicks only get in my way especially out of shape cohorts. I prefer collaborators. A good collaborator can remain almost invisible. As I wheel into the main entrance gate of the Medical Examiner's Office and turn off in ignition. A Security Guard comes out carrying bright pink high heel shoes.

"I hope those aren't his," remarks Captain West. "Listen. I don't think I know a Dr. Bhat," he again remarks.

I sat there holding my keys watching the Security Guard place the boots into the truck of a red Kia. As the guard passes a badge in front of an electronic key pad, "Dr. Bhat is Dr. Hussein's lab assistant, and I need to ask him a few more questions."

Captain West finally catches on, "Something didn't quite add up about the cause of death of Murdock?"

I continue watching the guard enter the building as we both get of the car. "You could say that." I glance and smile at Captain West, "If you're going to lie at least tell a logical lie that adds up and makes sense."

Captain West rings the buzzer of the electronic door. We could see the guard seeing at the desk through the glass window as the automatic doors opened and closed behind us. We already had our badges in our hand, and give the customary quick flash. The guard asks coldly, "What can I do for you."

"I need to see Dr. Bhat," I answer.

"They've been searching for Dr. Bhat since yesterday," replies the guard. He points to the clip board on the desk, and "I need you to sign in."

Captain West signs in first and then I pick up the clip board, and glance at the date and names and immediately notice, the date, Monday July 2, 2012. I glanced at the names and immediately I recognize one name, Tony Rome at signed in at 7:30 that morning. I ask, "He's missing?"

"He came in, but there is no record of him ever leaving the building…strangest thing I've ever seen," says the guard. The guard gets call on his, "We've found Dr. Bhat!

Captain West was relieved, "Good."

"Call the police," said the female voice on the radio.

The radio is attached to the shoulder of his uniform and push's the button on the shoulder of his radio, "I'm glad you found him…the police are here and they want to talk to Dr. Bhat."

The female voice, "Talking to him is going to be very difficult."

The guard smiles me as I lean on the edge of the tall desk and he asks, "Why is that?"

The female voice pauses, "We just found him in one of the meat lockers, dead."

Captain West and I glance at one another as the guard releases the button, "What in heck?" He rushes from behind the desk, "Follow me!" We take off running down a long hall as Captain West surprises everyone with his ability to keep up at a study pace.

CHAPTER 13

Undertaker, Brad Mosley

I don't know what's wrong with my son, Troy. "Listen. Death and taxes is the only certainty. You need to forget that Rasta-Dogg Rapper thing, and get into the one field that guaranteed to pay. Be an Undertaker. You can rap about that."

Troy looks down at the floorboard of the Hurst, then blurts out, "I love rapping...Dad I'm a great rapper."

"You rap while you're embalming." I tried to rhyme, "I'm the Undertaker. Death is a money maker. They'll be cold as ice, but I'll have them looking nice..."

Troy roars, "I'd rather be a Rapper!"

I continue my rhyme, "I not paying for that, and you bank on that."

I drive around to the back of the Medical Examiner's Office as Troy slumps down in the seat of the Hurst. Troy gets out and I watch as he gives me the various hand signals and I back the long white Hurst into the dock. I turn off the engine and grab my clip board and Troy opens the back hatch and pulls out the gurney, then slams the hatch shut. As we're walking I tell Troy, "You need to be the Grand Master of your time or you'll be a slave to it." Troy rings the bell as I look over the papers for the funeral arraignments.

Dr. Hussein's laboratory attendant, Kristen opens the door, and Troy rolls in the Gurney as

Kristen looks over Brad's forms. Kristen looks to be no more than eighteen and I can see her eyes salivating with hunger at Troy's long dreadlock's, sagging pants and long tee-shirt . Compound that with his over top good looks and you have formula no woman can say no to. I sign Medical Examiner's release forms for the remains of Raymond C. Murdock. Troy grips the end of the gurney as he looks at the many rolls and columns of lockers. "Everything is in order, let's go to locker seventeen" replies Kristen.

Kristen leads us down a long white sterile hallway and I notice a lot of activity a little further down the hall. Police and Crime Scene Investigator's crowd around like pigs headed to the slaughter of a roped off area. Troy glances at me and mumbles under his breath, "It's time to go."

I learned to stay calm a long time ago, and I communicated with a simple gesture of my hand, "And we'll be on our way soon," as we follow Kristen to locker seventeen. Kristen opens the locker and quickly pulls out the drawer.

On the table, a body covered by a sheet. Kristen pulls away the sheet revealing none of the external signs of an autopsy; such as stitches, lines and scars. Troy steps back from the gurney as Brad grabs the body by one leg and the arm and slides it onto his gurney and covers it with a flesh sheet. I hand Kristen my sheet, "I need Dr. Hussein to sign my release form before I can take the body."

"Yes I know…let me take your forms," I hand the forms to Kristen as I roll the gurney into the hallway. Troy and I watch as Kristen walks in the direction of the police activity. Detective Virginia Breeze comes out wearing latex gloves, Troy recognizes her immediately, "That's the Detective from television."

I watch Kristen as she stops at the roped off area and speaks to Detective Breeze. Detective looks dead at me before she walks back into the room and Dr. Hussein walks out. Dr. Hussein comes out into the hall and signs the forms Kristen is holding. He looks in my direction and waves, and I wave and nod. Kristen walks back in my direction and she escorts us onto the loading dock.

I leave Troy and Kristen with the body of Ray Murdock as Kristen opens the dock bay door and I back the Hurst completely in. With the press of a button the rear door of the Hurst opens and Troy slides the gurney on and I press another button and the gurney locks into place and Troy closes the rear door of the Hurst.

I watch from the side rearview mirror as Kristen and Troy walk out together. Kristen hands Troy a slip of paper, and he shoves it into his right pocket of his pants. Troy opens the car door and watch's Kristen as she walks into the building, and I assert, "Come boy. We've got to go!"

As the Hurst get onto the interstate 270 ramp, Troy turns on looks at the gurney. Troy yelled, "Dad he's sitting up!"

I respond in deep gruff voice, "Push him down." And explain, "It's just his nerves."

Troy snaps at his father, "His nerves! What about my nerves?"

"It's only natural reflexes...it happens sometimes. "When I make the pickups alone, they stay up until I get to the funeral home, then I push him back down." I instruct Troy," Just reach back there and push him down."

Troy extends his arm towards Deacon Murdock, but he is too scared and pulls his arm back, but Deacon Murdock lays back down on his own. "He just laid back down!"

Brad says, "That happens sometimes too."

Troy says, "I'm not sure I'm cut out to be an undertaker."

"Son, this is just your first time it'll get better and you'll be as good as anyone ever flipped burgers in a fast food restaurant."

From a distance, the large sign of B. Mosley Mortuary is visible. The mortuary looks like an old Southern Plantation Mansion. The Mortuary belonged to Brad father and grandfather. When his father died the family, business passed to Brad and his first cousin, Beulah Murdock. Beulah and her daughter Nichelle took care of all the burial arraignments for Ray Murdock, but of course a much lower rate than for a normal customer. People have no idea how affordable a funeral can be, but they get lost in their grief and lose sight of 3how much they are being charged. My policy, if the life insurance policy is worth fifty thousand dollars, then I sell them all the bells and whistles. We live on the third floor and the business takes up the entire first and second floor of the building. We all have a job in the funeral business. Charlene does deceased women's hair, makeup and nails on a part-time basis. Charlene owns a school of cosmetology known as Mosley Beauty Academy. Charlene brings her students in for training them in doing hair, makeup, and nails and other general duties having to do with the care of the dead. Troy is student in the Mortuary program at the local community college, and he gets straight A's. Troy's problems started when he began his internship at my funeral home. Brad dreams of Troy taking over the family business one day, but Troy dreams of becoming a rapper. Troy has done a few concerts with his buddy, T-Bogy, and they always draw a crowd wherever they do a concert on Friday and Saturday nights. I told Troy, "You need something you can fall back on in case that Rap thing doesn't work out, and undertaking is the one business that you'll never have to worry about being replaced by a computer or wait on people to download a CD."

Troy explains, to his dad, "There's this guy with a big record company from California and he wants us to sign with his record company." Troy's news falls on deaf ears as I place Ray's body on the embalming table in the Lab and look at my watch, "It almost dinner time, we'll get stated after dinner." Troy feeling relieved, takes a deep breath and rushes out the door and up the stairs.

Dinnertime is always a formal affair, and not by choice, but because of profession. Charlene always uses her best china and wine glasses. Even though no one drinks alcohol in the Mosley household, the wine glasses contain white grape juice or ice tea. Charlene regards dinner as family time, and dinner is never a simple menu, such a Fried Chicken, Macaroni and cheese and green beans. It's always over-the-top like tonight, Rice and Sage stuffed Pork Chops, broiled Zucchini slices, however, dessert is her specialty and everyone's favorite, Pineapple upside-Down Cake.

Shortly after dinner, I kiss Charlene on the cheek and inform her, "Great dinner, I'll have get another slice of cake later, but Troy and I have to get to work on Ray."

"It took them long enough to release his body." says Charlene. "A shame he drowned in the baptismal pool like that," and Charlene shakes her head.

Brad comments as, "The Death Certificate indicates poisoning."

Charlene lays her fork on her plate, wipes her mouth, "You mean someone, murdered him."

"It looks that way."

"I can't imagine anyone who would want to hurt Ray," says Charlene.

I had to clear my throat after that comment, "I would think anyone he's ever done business with."

Troy gets up from the table and picks up his plate, and was about to take it to the kitchen, and his mother interrupts, "Don't worry about that, help your father, I got this."

"Great," says a disappointed Troy.

We enter the lab and the table is empty. Troy looks around the room and no sign of Ray's body. I look in the walk in cooler for the remains of Ray Murdock and somehow I knew they would not be there. I walk around to the side entrance around the corner of the embalming lab and the side door is hanging off the hinges Troy suggests, "Maybe he walked off!"

I look around, "Nothing like this has ever happened before."

"Someone broke in and stole his body," responds Troy.

I frown, "Who would want to steal a dead body?"

I walk over to the land line phone hanging on the wall and dial, 9-1-1 and the emergency operator answers, "9-1-1 emergency."

Brad says, this is Brad Mosley of the B. Mosley Mortuary, and I'd like to report a body stolen."

The operator reluctantly asks, "Would you repeat that please?"

"This is Brad Mosley of B. Mosley Mortuary, and I'd like to report the body of Raymond Murdock has been stolen."

The operator says, "We will send a unit to your location."

Brad says, "Thank you."

CHAPTER 14

Detective Virginia Breeze

I feel like a hothouse tomato in this bio-hazard suit, but it's a necessary evil the entire Forensics Team must endure. My blinking cell phone hasn't stopped ringing. I'll let it ring until voicemail picks the call on the third ring. No sooner had my phone stopped ringing that Captain West's phone began ringing with the theme of Shaft. Captain West answers his phone then he steps out into the hallway away from Dr. Hussein.

I need to get a closer look at the man in locker seventeen and standing over him, without a doubt it was Dr. Ahmed Bhat. I ask Dr. Hussein, "What's your assessment?"

Dr. Hussein is bent over Dr. Bhat's body prodding and poking the forehead and skull like produce in a supermarket. "He couldn't be better preserved if he's been put in can like sardines." An orderly walks in and delivers a set of ex-rays to Dr. Hussein.

I would have thought the Medical Examiner's Office was more up to date and modernized, with CT Scans like many modern laboratories, but Dr. Hussein prefers to do things the old fashioned way.

Dr. Hussein holds the ex-ray up to the light, "Just as I thought. Looks like a .38, but I want know for certain until I fish the bullet out."

Dr. Hussein looks at the tools on the table, and he picks up a small electronic saw, "I'm about to remove the crown of the skull."

I've got nerves of steel, but not the stomach. I wanted to excuse myself, but Dr. Hussein must have seen a trace of apprehension on my face, but I'm determined to stick this out without hurling my guts onto the pavement.

The Chief of Security Operations, Kenneth Cox stands in the doorway motioning to me, "I need to speak to you," he tells me in a disturbingly animated tone.

You can look at some people and can't tell a thing about their character, but not Kenneth. Kenneth is an albino shaped Humpty Dumpty with a face full of freckles. Kenneth's the type of security guard that would give the untrained person the impression he's retired police officer. I've been around long enough to know that ole Humpty is mostly Dumpty. I know more about Kenneth than he realizes. I pulled off the blue latex gloves as I walked out into the hall, "Let me see what's on the surveillance camera."

"That's what I wanted to talk to you about," he pauses and continues, "All the cameras in this section of the building malfunctioned."

I knew if I were going to hit a snag it was going to be with the video surveillance equipment, "Take me to the area," I commanded.

He escorted me to a nearby office with a Do Not Enter sign posted on the door. I almost expected state of the art surveillance equipment, but not this place. I couldn't believe it. I am looking at a cheap wooden cabinet with a VCR inside.

Captain West comes into the room talking on his cell phone, "Yeah. We'll be right over."

One look at this security setup and you'll know this is a long way from being a NASA Pre-launch inspection. Captain West walks over and opens the cabinet and bends over to take a closer look, "They still make VCR's?"

He picks up the remote control and presses the stop button and nothing happened. I stuck my finger into the machine to see whether or not there was a type inside, "Empty."

Captain West asks, "Where's the VHS type?"

I looked at my finger, and it was covered with dust. "This machine hasn't been used for a long time and you said the equipment malfunctioned!"

Two more security guards came into the room and from the looks of them they should have retired years ago.

It's not my intent to get under ole Humpty's skin and as Kenneth stammered to find the right words, "We've had some special problems that involve cuts in budget." I simply stated, "I'll be speaking to the director to discuss the lapse in security."

Kenneth raised his voice, "This is a morgue! People don't normally go out their way to commit homicide in a MORGUE!"

Captain West told ole Dumpty, or should I say Kenneth that, "If I were you, I'd clean out my desk."

Kenneth and the two guards leave the room and I had an idea, "I saw a bank across the street."

"Maybe there's something on their tape," asserted Captain West.

I attempted to raise an objection, "I'm not sure we'll gain access."

Captain West frowned, "Banks can be a little funny about getting involved with anything that does not have anything to do with bank robbery." Captain West looks directly at me and suggests, "Maybe you and some of your NSA friends can pull some strings."

I remember the last time I had dealings with a bank; in fact, it was the Federal Reserve Bank and that was an experience I don't care to repeat. "Possibly, but I can't make any promises."

Captain West replies, "Fine, but in the meantime we need to Head over to B. Mosley Mortuary."

I hate funeral homes. I always have a very bad attitude regarding funeral homes and undertakers.

Captain West has a very impersonal viewpoint when I come's to stating the facts, "There has been a body snatching."

"I know the funeral home and the location in the City of St. Louis." Captain West stood there looking at me smiling as I told him, "I grew up in that neighborhood and they may be capable of a lot of things but, "Someone stole a dead body?"

In my line of work I expect almost anything, but "This has got to be a first."

His eyes met mine and he sighed, "Someone came in and stole the body of Ray Murdock," said Captain West.

CHAPTER 15

Chief of Police, Darnell Logan

Drug deals that have taken a wrong turn down a dead end street, the unfaithful wife or husband are counted among the dearly departed, Ice Cream trucks that sell more than just Popsicle's, these are open and closed cases the majority of the time. But, every once in a while there will be a case that is so far outside the box that it breaks the mold and the Ray Murdock is that kind of case.

I and Commissioner, Richard Horton are twenty-five year veterans of the police force, but to look at us now we are a couple of three hundred pound mammoth's unable to run from the conference room to the water cooler and that's while being chased. I say the heck with it, shoot and ask questions later.

Commissioner Horton walks in carrying a box with two foot long submarine sandwiches, chips and two Diet Cola's to wish it down. We prefer wishing rather than washing because we wish all the fat wouldn't settle around our middle. We dig right into the box begin gorging ourselves. "We need to bring the Murdock case to a close."

I explain, "The Medical Examiner is still trying to figure out what poison was used."

Commissioner Horton's motto is: "Why take the time to read the report when someone's willing to tell you what's in the report." He stops in the middle of a bite and looks at me like I'm dead crazy, "I thought Murdock drowned?"

I looked at the double ham, beef and cheese on my sandwich and attempted to go through my song and dance of explanations, "He did, but had he not drowned he would have died from being poisoned."

"Reverend Shawn Graves and his church are well connected and I've got attorneys from New York and California breathing down my neck," rants Commissioner Horton as he looks at his watch, "Captain West is supposed to be her."

I was about to take a bite and paused, "He's doing field work with Detective Breeze." I took a momentary pause, "There's been a new development in the Murdock case."

He glances up from his sandwich at me, "Oh yeah?"

"Captain West and Detective Breeze went on a call at B. Mosley Mortuary regarding a missing body." I take a quick bite of my sandwich as a delay tactic.

Commissioner Horton squint's his eyes and frowns, "Excuse me."

"The body of Ray Murdock has been stolen," I murmured aloud.

Commissioner Horton begins his tirade, "What does this get filed under lost and found, robbery, or a body snatching. Wait until the News Media gets hold of this, then the departmental cost is going to make it extremely difficult to keep the NSA operation secret and we better hope the media doesn't get wind of it!"

"As I see it we don't have much of a choice," I respond.

With a mouth full of food and ranting like he's got Mad Cow Disease, "The Mayor shoved Agent Virginia Breeze and the NSA down our flipping throat!"

My feelings are no secret to Mayor Joel Golden and the Police Commissioner, "I don't like the idea of our having no idea of what she's working on and she's not required to answer to either of us."

Somewhat calm, "I know. It has a very bad stench. To squelch any hint suspicion, we'll keep playing along."

I scarfed down the last bite, "Absolutely, and at the first opportunity..."

Commissioner Horton has a renewed sense of authority he cuts me off mid-sentence, "Get rid of Agent Virginia Breeze." He places the sandwich wrapper into the empty potato chip bag then tosses it NBA style into the wastebasket across the room.

There is get of rid of her. Then there is, GET RID OF HER. I learned not to ask too many questions long ago, but some matters are best decided by making the best educated guess and hope for the best. At the end of the day, it does not make any difference how we get rid of her as long as it gets done.

CHAPTER 16

Detective Virginia Breeze

There is a swarm of police squad cars, crime scene vans, and a plain unmarked van with U.S. Government issue plates parked in front B. Mosley Mortuary on Natural Bridge Road. Television News trucks have found their spot directly across the street at the Knights of the Black Circle Lodge Parking lot. Since its private property and they paid to park, the police had no luck in forcing them to leave. When I looked at the black van I knew immediately who it was and I inform Captain West, "ATF guys."

Captain West says, "That explains Natural Bridge being hey had closed for the last three hours."

The ATF gave the all clear signal minutes prior to our arrival. If you've ever driven on Natural Bridge Road, then you already know that it stays busy twenty four seven. In St. Louis word of any major crime makes three rounds on the streets before it even hits the evening news, and the news traveled on the street at the speed of light of a body stolen from B. Mosley Mortuary.

Brad, Troy, Captain West and I are sitting in Brad's office as I begin my preliminary investigation. Brad's office is what must be the standard funeral director office. Along one of the walls I see several small scale models of coffins. They are small enough to fit into a doll house. I decided to keep it simple, "When did you notice the body missing?"

Brad answers, "Troy and I came down after dinner to prepare the body, and that's when we noticed it was missing."

Troy adds more detail to the events of the evening, "We searched the entire area and that's when we noticed the side door."

Captain West looks at Troy's baggy pants and long dreadlock's with complete contempt and his contempt is matched only by his question, "What made you think you had to look anyplace other than where you left the body?"

Troy smiles politely in my direction, "Well you see...on the way here Ray Murdock sat up straight in back of the Hurst, so I thought if he could sit up then he could get up and walk off like a Zombie."

I did my best to hold back a laugh, but I managed a smile, and suggest to Troy, "You're not really interested in being an Undertaker? Are you?"

Before Troy could answer his Father, Brad suggests, "Troy? Why don't you go upstairs and check on your mother? Without another word, Troy exits the room.

Captain West and I are escorted through the funeral home by Brad Mosley. We pass through a room of coffins of various designs, sizes colors. Like cadavers have toe tags, so coffin had a price tag hanging out of the foot of each coffin. Captain West stops to look at a solid gold plated coffin with a blank name plate at the head, "Nice," He looks at the price tag of seventy thousand dollars, "Christ Jesus! Bet you've been holding that a while?"

Brad glances at the coffin, "That's a special order that arrived three weeks ago."

I comment to Captain West and Brad, "Guess the customer changed their mind?"

In a cold professional tone, "Mrs. Murdock ordered it several months ago."

Brad is about to continue to his embalming lab and I demanded an explanation, "Ray Murdock was still alive three weeks ago!"

70

I insisted, "You said Mrs. Murdock ordered it special?"

Brad continued, "It's not unusual for our more wealthy customers to make pre-burial arraignments.

My replied hostilely, "Yeah. Just before they turn up dead?"

Captain West, "Something stinks around here and it's not the stiffs."

CHAPTER 17

Detective Virginia Breeze

We were led through a maze of rooms and refrigeration units. It feels like we have been walking through this maze of death forever and Captain West whispers, "Any day now." Brad Mosley heard him to my surprise, and Brad informed us, "Almost there."

Brad opened the door and we enter the embalming lab, but the Hydraulic Operating Table with a burgundy cover on the floor drew my attention. I looked at the cloth and asked, "What's this?"

"That is a First Call Cover. It's used to cover the remains" Brad answers.

I see various body lifters and transfer devices hanging overhead, but the machine in the corner drew my attention next. The machine looks like a blender, and again I ask, "What that?"

Without going into anything technical he says, "Porti-Boy Embalming Machine."

I begin opening the various cabinets and see different types of chemicals used in the embalming process. I look at the Undertaker and ask, "Any chemicals missing?"

Brad came over and looked at all the chemicals, "Nothing is missing." He proceeds to opening another cabinet with even more chemical's and adhesives, "Everything is..." He looks at the boxes of various adhesives, "There are several boxes missing."

Captain West presses Brad, "What's missing"

Brad looks at me and replies, "Thanoseal Flesh is missing."

I ask, "What's it used for?"

I remove a small notepad from the pocket of my black Armani Leather Jacket as Brad describes in detail the purpose of the Thanoseal Flesh, "It makes damaged human flesh look natural, but I would've had to use it on Ray Murdock because he had no cuts, scars, burns and gunshot wounds that require a more natural looking human flesh."

I scrutinized the various surgical tools on a stainless steel tray setting on a cart next to the Hydraulic Operating Table. I observed another tray of plastic tubes and a case of plastic bags.

In all my years as an investigator, this is the first time I've ever been on the seen a mortician's lab and the tools of the trade. Captain West looked at the box of plastic bags and inquires, "What the bags for?"

Brad stood watching and waiting for the next question, "Those are used to store body parts."

Captain West simply replies, "Aha…Okay?"

I ask, "You incinerate them on site?"

Brad replies, "No. They are stored at the foot of the casket and buried with the body."

I am stunned to learn this kind of detail, "Really?"

Brad continues, "Haven't you ever heard old cops use the phrase, this case is in the bag?"

Captain West looked at Brad strangely and said, "I heard people say that, but I had no idea this is what they meant."

Without moving, I looked around the room for anything that might seem out of place and I notice a cubby hole of a doorway that looks as though it leads nowhere and as I point in the general direction I ask, "Where does that lead?"

"It leads down another passageway," Brad leads the way, "Come and I will show you."

It is a narrow entryway that makes a shape turn into the Embalming room from the driveway of the Mortuary. The door is hanging off its hinges. There are a group of men wearing military clothing with enormous letters that read, ATF. A tall man with blond hair and blue eyes wearing an ATF jacket walks up to Virginia and introduces himself, "I'm Agent Frank Masterson. After a brief pleasantry, Agent Masterson hands me a piece of soft white putty and I begin pinching it between my thumb and forefinger and Masterson explains, "We found small traces of explosives like what you're holding."

I immediately stop pinching it and looked at it and Captain West responds, "OMFG...WTF?"

I try to pass the C4 putty to Captain West, and he yells, "I don't want it!"

Agent Masterson took the sample and I ask, "I'm surprised it didn't take the entire build out?"

The Undertaker, Brad Mosley is standing to the side, and he informs me, "Detective Breeze I have the funeral service for Alonzo Simmons in one of the chapels that I need to attend to."

Captain West remembers, "That's kid was killed in the drive-by shooting last week."

Brad answers, "Yes."

I looked at him, "Of course go right ahead" and Brad Mosley leaves.

"This was a low level charge and this guy knew what he was doing," states Masterson as he points at the door frame and hinges.

Captain West asserted, "You mean this guy is military?"

"The culprit could be, but I seriously doubt it," he says as shrugs his shoulders.

I smiled at Masterson and inquire jokingly, "I've have the feeling you know something."

"That's very intuitive of you Detective Breeze," as he hands me a flirtatious grin like he's handing me chocolate.

Captain West can be very impatient, "You two can play kiss face another time because I don't have the time!"

Agent Masterson steps closer to Captain West, forcing Captain West to look up as Masterson explains, "Demolition Companies use C4 and other types of explosives in the construction trade."

Finally everyone is on the same page and so to confirm my understanding, "So we're looking for someone that may have worked in construction or demolition?"

"That's a big affirmative," replied Agent Masterson.

I look at the door and hinges meticulously, "Wouldn't this have made a loud noise that would have been heard?" and after I ask that question we heard the sound of a car backfiring with a loud, "BOMB!"

There is the sound of a loud rhythmic beating of a car stereo, and Captain West comments, "Must be Satan's Heartbeat."

Agent Masterson, "Yes, but as you can hear, other background sounds can camouflage any low level explosions."

"Yeah I've got the point," but as busy as Natural Bridge is I know someone saw a dead body being carried out.

"I want to point out that there was a Construction Company that had a break in at one of their supply buildings several months ago," informs Agent Masterson.

Captain West shakes his head, "Let me guess...Murdock Construction?"

"You got it. Murdock Construction and Demolition, Inc.," responds Masterson as he hands me his business card at the ATF. He smiles, "Just in case you need anything,"

The three of us walk outside and onto the sidewalk. We watch the crowd of young people gathering on the sidewalk as we stop on the

sidewalk to talk. Suddenly, a black sports car with dark tinted windows slows down near the crowd. We watch as the window is rolled down and in automatic response Masterson and I pull our weapons at the same time as a man in a grey hoodie fires shots from an AK-47 into the crowd. Three people are hit including Captain West. Masterson and I return fire. The shooter falls in the direction of the driver. I'm sure both I and Masterson hit the shooter in the shoulder and chest. Agent Masterson continues firing off rounds and his last shoot shatters the back windshield as the car speeds away, "No tags!" yells Masterson.

CHAPTER 18

Lisa West

Lisa West is the fifty-three year old wife of Cornelius West and they have been married for twenty-seven years. They have an eighteen year old daughter, Shonease. I knew what profession he worked in and the risks that are part of the job. When he was a street cop when we first married and I worried constantly. As he began working himself up the latter became less apprehensive because he remains at the precinct the majority of time. Cornelius was promoted to Captain a couple of years ago and it was at that stage of his career he decided he needed to be more closely connected to his officers and their day to day duties as street cops. My life was worry free until he started doing his random ride-a-along once a month with one of his officers.

I was about to plug in the vacuum cleaner when the monthly emergency test sirens cried out. I continued to vacuum the floor. Between the vacuum cleaner and the sirens I didn't hear the doorbell or the telephone ringing. When the emergency sirens completed their test I heard a loud banging on the door. I yelled, "One moment please!" I turned off the vacuum and the telephone was ringing. The banging continued as I decided to answer the phone first, "Hello...Oh my God!" I hung up the phone and rushed to the door to find Virginia Breeze and two police cars.

I opened the door and Virginia rushes in and I ask in complete panic, "What happened?"

Virginia said, "Come on and I explain on the way!"

I grabbed my purse and Virginia and I left with one police car in front of us and another behind. Our motorcade zoomed though every through every stop sign, red light and major intersection.

Cornelius and I knew Virginia before she became connected with the NSA. Virginia tells me, "He was airlifted to St. Matthew's Hospital after the shooting."

I could feel the tears welling up, "What exactly happened?"

"We went to B. Mosley Mortuary to investigate a case," replied Virginia.

I could help myself, but I had to interrupt, "That Ray Murdock case?"

"Yes. Captain West's shooting had nothing to do with the Murdock case," Virginia paused for a moment as she makes a sharp turn into Kingshighway, "At this point I don't think so."

I could tell from the tone of her voice she didn't believe that story any more than I did, but I held my tongue. My thoughts were on Cornelius and my daughter, Shonease. I took out my cell phone called and there was no answer, and commented, "Pick up for heaven's sake." He voicemail picked

up, "Shonease come to St. Matthews Hospital. You father's been shot," I spoke into her voice mail.

Virginia asks, "Where is she?"

I said, "She's probably with her boyfriend, Troy."

"That's the second time today I've heard the name Troy," said Virginia as she squalls her tires as she makes a sharp turn into the emergency entrance of St. Matthew's Hospital.

"You should. Troy is the son of Brad Mosley," I said.

CHAPTER 19

Knights of the Black Circle

"Time is important and of the essence" proclaims the Sovereign from the front of an altar. The Sovereign identity is a closely guarded secret as is the membership of the Knights of the Black Circle. The Sovereign is wearing black hooded cloak with a golden lion stitched on the front. There are seventy people gathered in the secret catacombs of the Knights of the Black Circle building and they are wearing solid black cloaks.

A man enters wearing a gray hoodie and he lays his gun upon the altar, "It is done," he said. The man stood at attention as if awaiting orders.

The Sovereign's phone rang, "Yes. Yes. Yes. I understand." He turns to the man in the gray hoodie, "You weren't to injure any bystanders and no one was to identity you."

"They go into the way," and they he walks away and kneels in front of the seventy members.

The Sovereign's cell phone rings again, "Yes," then he puts the cell phone into the pocket of his cloak. He points to the young man in the gray hoodie and picks up the gun from the altar with a glove gloved hand and asks, "Are you ready to be initiated Apostle?"

He stands and faces the leader with his hand folded in prayer, "I am ready," said the man in the gray hoodie gets up and faces the Sovereign Leader, "Lay on the altar.

CHAPTER 20

The Apostle lay's down on the altar and a group of eleven people join the leader and surround the altar. A large theatrical screen lowers itself in front of the membership. There is a complete view of the activities within the circle for all to see. The Sovereign Leader says, "You have failed in your mission."

The Apostle yells, "No way. I saw Captain West fall dead!"

"He lives," said the Sovereign Leader.

"He lives," chanted the eleven around th altar. "You failed," chanted the other members. The Apostle realizes he may be in trouble and tries to get up from the altar and the eleven hold him down as he beseeches the Sovereign for mercy, "Forgive me...I...I can make this right!"

The Sovereign puts his hand on the Apostle shoulder in an attempt to calm him, "You're forgiven."

"You're forgiven," chants the eleven.

"Make him an example," chants the membership.

The Sovereign Leader reaches under the altar and pulls out a black wool sack and someone wearing a red hooded cloak comes over carrying a bright yellow and red snake and places the snake in the bag and the Apostle eyes fill with terror, "I thought he was dead!"

The eleven held him down as the person in the red cloak comes over chanting, "Blessed is the silence," and he stuffs a giant sponge into the apostle's mouth to muffle his screams.

The members chant in unison, "Blessed be the silence!"

The Sovereign Leader whispers into the Apostle's ear, "You are forgiven." The words are amplified and echoed by the sound system, "You are forgiven"

The Apostle calms down and the eleven release him. Suddenly, the Sovereign Leader slips the open end of the black sack over the Apostle's head and tightens the ends.

He screams and squirms to no avail until there is silence and he lays motionlessness and limp.

CHAPTER 21

Detective Virginia Breeze

Lisa West, Commissioner Horton and Chief Wilson and a host of uniformed police officer wait outside the Urgent Care Unit of St. Matthews Hospital. Shonease sits next to her mother, Lisa and Troy stands next to Shonease.

A man wearing blue surgical scrubs comes out, "Mrs. Cornelius West?"

Lisa and Shonease rush to the doctor, "Right here!"

"Hello, I'm Dr. Thomas."

Commissioner Horton and Chief Wilson walk's over and stand next to Lisa, "How is he?"

"Captain West will be fine. Good thing he was wearing his vest otherwise, I would have been must worse."

Everyone breaths a sign of relief and Shonease asks, "Can I go in and see my Dad?"

Everyone was paying close attention to Dr. Thomas, "The vest caught the bullet. He just has a couple of bruised ribs. We'll need to keep him overnight to observation."

"Like hell you are!" Everyone turns to see Captain West standing in the middle of the floor in a hospital gown.

Lisa looks smiles at Cornelius, "No problem."

Captain West yells, "Where's my clothes?

CHAPTER 22

Denisha Logan

People think I got it made just because my father is Chief of Police, Darnell Logan. But, let me tell you this, who I am may have gotten me in the door, but it is my abilities that keep my here. I have not been handed anything on a silver platter. If anything, I have to work much harder and constantly keep proving myself to others especially my boss, Tom Johnson.

There are people that get employment through more modern channels while others less conventional channels. In Tom Johnson's case it was a questionable channel. How do you explain an unqualified department head? I'll tell you, but on second thought I won't tell you. Some people sleep their way to the top, but that is not the case with Tom Johnson, Tom could not get his dog to sleep with him. I normally work days, but sometimes my job requires an occasional evening and this is one of those evenings. I work for the police department, but I am not a law enforcement officer. I am a Network Intelligence Specialist and I investigate crimes involving computer networks.

A large utility truck pulls up behind my car on the parking lot of the main precinct and I glance out my rearview mirror and see that it is D'Metric Klein. We have been seeing one another for about two months and my father is the only reason I still see him. Daddy always tells me, "Troy does not have a J-O-B and D'Metric got a good job working for the electric company."

Troy and I broke up and he's seeing Captain West's daughter, Shonease. Let me tell you, Captain West is not happy about it. What I like about D'Metric is he is very gullible and I need that right now in order to get something done.

I get out of my car and look up at the normally pretty skyline or St. Louis, but tonight it is humid and cloudy. I climb into D'Metric's truck and we snuggle and talk, "I need you to do this and I want ask for anything else."

D'Metric responds reluctantly, "It's too risky and what if we get caught?"

"It'll take fifteen minutes and you flip the power back on," I instruct him with a devious smile, "I make it worth your while."

Unenthusiastically, D'Metric agrees, "I'll wait five minutes and then turn the power back on."

There is a distant clash of thunder as I happily smile at D'Metric, "Thank you. Thank you." I happily jump out of the truck, and fling my heavy knapsack over my shoulder.

D'Metric leans down in my direction and holds his hand up to me, "Five minutes."

"That's all I'll need and I may not need that much time," D'Metric.

I slam the door shut and I watch D'Metric do a perfect U-Turn in his big white Utility Truck on the crowded parking lot. This lot is always crowded with cars even though there may not be that many people in the building. I hear another clash of thunder, but it seems a little closer this time as I rush into the building.

I see my boss Tom standing in the hall talking to a Network Administrator as I walk into my office and close the door. My office door is the only door with a lock and Tom hates it. This used to be his office, but because of the sensitive nature of my work, he was forced to give up his office so I could have it and he has to work out of a cubical like almost everyone else. Tom has had it in for me from that point on.

I quickly unzipped my bag and crawled under my desk to connect my computer and the network server to the portable battery generator. The last step is to power up and wait for the completion of the start-up routine. While I wait I hear a knock at the door and I know who it is. I tuck everything under my desk and out of eye shot before I got up to open the door, "Hay what's up."

"I didn't realize you were working tonight," says Tom.

"We've had a lot of system problems and I need to get caught up on a few things," I explained.

"I'm upgrading the software on the primary systems, and it's going to take all night," said Tom and without much thought he added, "Your system is not connected on the same server as everyone else's at the moment."

Tom has been trying to get access to my server with little success since day one, so if he thinks he will wire my system to his well I've got a surprise for him. There was a momentary pause between the two of us before Tom finally breaks the silence, "Your system will be connected directly to the main network by morning."

I demand, "By whose authorization?"

Tom clears his throat, "The new network subcontractor, DataSpink."

"I'll need to talk to the Government agencies whom this system belongs to before I can give you access because you don't have the security clearance."

"Too late now," laughs Tom.

I looked down in disbelief, "I'll let you take that up with the FBI, ATF and Homeland Security, but for now you're not getting access."

Tom turns to leave, but stops and turns back to me, "I almost forgot to mention that we already got access to your office via the floor tiles."

I looked down at the white floor tile. It the kind used in computer rooms. All you need is a double floor plunger to pull them up. I felt as though someone has just dropped a grenade in my lap. I looked up at the ceiling tiles.

Tom says, "Yes. We went that way also," and he continues, "You see? You may have drove me out of my office, but you'll never have my job, the power or the authority."

At every turn, Tom tries to run me over, but I refuse to let him get the best of me.

I look at my system and it is waiting at the login screen and Tom comes in again, but he does not knock like he did the first time.

"I want you off my system in five minutes, so the new software can download." He slams the door as he leaves.

I begin to login and suddenly the building loses power, "Thank you D'Metric I owe you one."

Quickly typing and going through various access points to gain access to locked criminal files of

from Interpol," OMG! Virginia's not going to believe this." I pull a small Data Storage device out of my bag and popped it into the small slot in from of the computer. I copy everything.

Tom begins banging on my door, "Open up!"

The little blue light flashed on the Data Storage Device as it copied each file and Tom continued banging like a madman at my door, "Open up or I'll have it broken down!"

Staring at the computer screen, "Hurry," I said. "Hurry up." A message displayed on the screen, ALL FILES COPIED SUCCESSFULLY! I pulled out the data stick and shoved it down my bra. I logged out of the computer and crawled under the desk and disconnected the computer from the portable generator and back into the sockets in the wall.

Tom is still banging and yelling at the door, "Denishia, open this door!"

I hang the bag on my shoulder and opened the door, "What's happened to the electricity?"

Tom rushes into my office and looks at my computer, "What were you doing?"

This is the way I planned it, and D'Metric was right on time. I ask, "I wonder why the diesel generator didn't kick in?"

Tom started pressing the keys on the keyboard to no avail, but he had already decided that I was up to something.

I said, "I lost everything I was working on!"

Tom tried to play off his suspicions, "That's why you should keep saving every three to five lines."

I turn to leave and Tom looks at me, "Where do you think you're going?"

"Home," I said and turned and left.

CHAPTER 23

Denishia Logan

As soon as I began taking direct orders from Virginia and the NSA, I knew Tom would be a problem and so he is. I lost no time getting out of that building. I have enough flexibility in my work that it matters very little where I do my work, but that the work gets done.

My iPhone keeps sounding my all too familiar ringtone; <u>I shot the Sheriff,</u> by Eric Clapton. That's the ringtone for my boss Tom and my iPhone has been ringing and beeping since I left the office. Ordinarily it would take thirty minutes or more to get home, but Tom scared the Bajesus out of me and I put the pedal-to-the-floor and got out of there. I glance around at the crowded parking lot of the Chow Mein House and I throw the Jeep into park and turned off the ignition. I started to go to D'Metric's, but I can't because his system is not setup for my work, so that gives me little choice. Retrieve the files and forward the information to Virginia A.S.A.P. The Chow Mein House is a little hole in the wall Chinese

Restaurant located at the corner of Kingshighway and Delmar Boulevard and it has the best Asian food in St. Louis. Chow Mein House has a small Plexiglas order window that is just big enough for the cashier to pass your order through.

There is a large refrigeration unit visible that stocked full of every flavor of Vess Soda known to man and as always I always order my favorites, the <u>Vess Whistle Orange Soda</u> with a half order of Pork Fried Rice, Crib Rangoon and one Egg Roll. The cashier rings up my order of $12.46.

The cashier, Sue has been working here for many years and I can't tell how old she is, but Sue was working here when my Grandmother was a high school student at Baumont in the 1970's.

Sue reads my order back to me in broken English, "Half order Pork Fried Rice, one Crib Rangoon and one Egg Roll."

"Yes," I say.

I always order the same thing and the total is always the same, "Your order come to $12.46."

I hand Sue three five dollar bills, and I hear the ring of the register and see the draw pop open and with the speed and agility of a professional bank teller, Sue counts out my exact change, "Two dollar and fifty-four cent you change." Sue tears off my receipt and gives me one part and she keeps the other as she yells my order in Mandarin to the male cook in the kitchen and he yells something back to her. Sue tells me, "Your number three-o-two and will be twenty minute."

A slightly bald man in his fifties, wearing kaki pants and a St. Louis Cardinal's T-Shirt with construction boots is leaning against the wall marketing a lottery play slip. A young man in his twenties wearing black sagging jeans and an oversized T-shirt walks over to him and comments, "I don't know why you're wasting your time on that crap because know body ever wins from this neighborhood."

A young woman walks over pushing a baby stroller with a newborn baby inside and holding the hand of a two year boy, dives into the conversation like an Olympic Swimmer drives from a board, "Better save it for the boat." Everyone laughs and the woman asks the man with the Lottery Play Slip, "What's the jackpot up to?"

The man pauses and answers, "It's back down to twenty million."

The young man asks, "You mean someone had the ticket last Saturday Night."

"Yeah," says the man as he continues marking play slips.

The young man in the sagging black jeans remarks, "It wasn't me!"

"Me either," yells Sue from behind the Plexiglas window.

The young man in the sagging pants turns to Sue and asks, "You play the lottery?"

Sue snaps at him, "You think I want do this the rest my life? I want live on easy street just like you!"

The entire restaurant burst in laughter as a middle aged Asian man walks over to Sue and says something to her in Mandarin Chinese and sits a bag on the counter, then walks away. Sue yells, "Three-o-Two!"

After all that I almost forgot my number and had to check my ticket, "Oh. That's me." I pick up my bags and exit the restaurant until my next visit.

Arriving home and taking a shower, Denishia is sitting alone on the floor surrounded by pillows, and with open container of Pork Fried Rice, and a little bag of Crab Rangoon.

She has a notebook computer sitting on her lap. She reaches into her bra and takes out the Data Storage device and inserts the data storage device into the port while taking a bite of an egg roll. She brings up the files.

The first file has a picture at the beginning of the files, and personal information, shows the file juvenile dating back to eighteen years prior. He was sixteen, and the file indicates he was a member of the street gang, the Disciples. The police reports on the night of April 11, 1997 the police pulled Shawn over for speeding, but a search of the vehicle all three occupants, all male to be carrying crack

cocaine and an assortment of pills. Two were initially charged as adults and Shawn was charged as a Juvenile.

Even though Shawn Graves had drugs on him, all charges were later dropped. But I was surprised to learn that the original arresting officer was Captain Cornelius West. I was suddenly startled when the doorbell rang. It seems especially loud and it sounded like it tolled from a bell tower rather than the door.

The clock on the mantle chimes eleven times as Denishia gets up off the floor and looks at the clock, "Who on earth would come visit anyone this time of the night?"

The doorbell rings again, and she yells, "Coming!"

As she walks toward the door a male voice yells, "Open up or I will break it down!"

Denishia quickly turns around and returns to the living room floor and knells down in front of the computer and begins to quickly type. She came hears the sound of someone ramming at her door, "BOOM! BOOM! BOOM!"

Denishia quickly turns her head in the direction of the front door before returning her gaze at the computer screen. She quickly types in Virginia Breeze's NSA email address and sends all the files from the Data Storage Device as an attachment. She hits the return key on the keyboard and waits what seems like an eternity before a message is displayed and a voice automated responder says, "Your mail has been sent to Virginia Breeze."

She quickly pulls out the small storage device as she hears a loud crush of her front door. She clinches the device in her fist and she runs through the house and to the back door. She bursts out the back door and takes off like a sprinter toward the back parking lot. Denishia pulls her keys from her pocket and jumps into her Jeep and she sees two men run from her apartment, one is her boss Tom Johnson and the other was a man she recognized from one of the pictures from the Data Storage Device, "Holy crap! He's supposed to be dead!" Tom and the man looked around the parking lot and saw Denishia sitting in the Jeep and they come to a dead stop.

Denishia inserts the key into the ignition and she mumbles to herself, "I wonder why they stopped?" She continues staring at the men and Tom looks at her and does a four fingered wave and a fierce angry grin as she turns the key in the ignition. She hears a loud click and a pop and she cries out, "Christ Jesus," and the Jeep explodes.

The Man with Tom Johnson only response as they walk away, "He's not here tonight." People gather and sworn like bees trying to get a look at the burning car.

CHAPTER 24

Dr. Benjamin Hussein

"This is Dr. Benjamin Hussein and I have before me the body of Miss. Jean Newton, and a full autopsy will be completed to determine the cause of death," he speaks into the hanging microphone and camera. The camera show a full body shot of the nude body of Jean Newton. Dr. Hussein is interrupted by the ringing of his iPhone. He speaks into the microphone, "Camera off,' and the television screen fades to black in an instant.

He walks over to a contaminated waste bin and pulls off his latex gloves and surgical gown and discards them. Dr. Hussein pulls his iPhone from his belt clip and looks at the Caller ID and takes a deep breath and sighs, "Dr. Hussein."

A female voice with a thick Harvard Accent comes onto the line, "Hello. This is Dr. Dana Khan."

Dr. Hussein walks into his office and sits down and takes out a blank notepad and pen, "Nice of you to call and congratulations on the Nobel Prize in Botany."

"Thank you very much, but the reason for my call is I was contacted by a colleague of yours and mind, Dr. Bhat and I was hoping to speak with him, but I have been unsuccessful with contacting his exchange."

Dr. Hussein is doodling pictures of trains on the yellow pad, "I hate to be the one to inform you, but Dr. Bhat is dead."

Dr. Khan is taken aback, "That's unbelievable. What happened?"

As he continues doodling trains with greater detail he draws wings on the train, "Yes it is. He was murdered."

"I'm sorry to hear that," she tells Dr. Hussein.

In an attempt to shift the conversation, Dr. Hussein asks, "Have you made any progress with the poison?"

"Yes I have. Since I will be in St. Louis Speaking at Washington University I thought we could schedule a time to meet so I could go over the results with you," she tells him.

Dr. Hussein immediately stops doodling and puts the pen in his pocket, "That would be excellent, but for now what did you come up with?"

"The plant is native to the Amazon region," she said.

He pulls the pen out of his pocket and asks, "Can it be grown anywhere?"

"Only in a controlled environment and an experienced botanist," she informs him.

Dr. Hussein's call waiting beeped and there is a momentary silence on the line as Dr. Hussein looks at the screen of his iPhone. The name reads, XRX-XXX-XXXQ. Dr. Khan is still on the line, "Are you there?"

He answers, "Yes. Sorry."

She comments, "I was afraid the call dropped. You know how inflight calls can be?"

He is surprised, "Inflight? Where are you?"

"On a flight from France and I will be landing in Los Angeles in two hours and I should be in St. Louis early tomorrow morning," said Dr. Khan.

Dr. Hussein thinks hard squints his eyes, "I wonder why it didn't turn up in the U.S. Government's Poison Center Information database?"

Dr. Khan's voice begins fading in and out, "It's not something currently used and it's not widely known. It is very difficult to extract."

"That explains a lot." he tells her.

"No one has seen this plant since 1938 and they thought it to be extinct," said Dr. Khan.

"Listen. Dr. Khan. This is evidence in a homicide investigation and if you can keep a lid on it. I'll see about getting you some samples."

With a sense of urgency in her voice, "There is something you need to know...Whatever you do. Do not," the iPhone goes completely dead.

Dr. Hussein looks at his iPhone and realizes that he forgot to recharge it the day before, "That's just great!"

CHAPTER 25

Detective Virginia Breeze

Captain West and Police Chief Darnell Logan's squalling tires announced their arrival on the scene of the back parking lot of Denishia's Loft Apartment. They both come to a complete stop in back of my car. The Fire Department, Bomb Squad and ATF are among the first responders on the scene of the car bombing. NSA Agent, Christian Kane arrived on the scene ten minutes after the influx of neighborhood spectators.

Chief Logan leaps himself in the direction of Denishia's still smoldering car. Like a strong gust of wind Captain West and several officers take hold of the powerfully built man. Chief Logan has a strong and rock-hard face with very prominent beaten down brow and bald head. Chief Logan is a man of action and at the moment he is all too ready for an all-out dogfight. He calls out to his daughter, Denishia! Denishia!

Captain West released his grip on Chief Logan, "You can help Denishia more by letting them do their job!"

Christian and I walked over to Chief Logan and at once Chief Logan lunged at Christian and clutched his throat, "This is your fault! My daughter should have never been involved with your NSA crap!"

Captain West forces Chief Logan to release his chokehold on Christian Kane, "The order trickled down from a higher authority than me!"

During the commotion no one noticed that the firefighters had stopped hosing down the car. I stepped closer to look through the charred window, but all I could see was the faint shadow of the driver. No one saw Commissioner Horton when he arrived and before I knew anything he was standing next to me. He only needed a split second look and he turned to Chief Logan, "Come on let's get out of her."

Chief Logan yelled, "I'm not leaving my daughter!"

"This is not a request, but an order. Detective Breeze has got this covered. Let's get out of here," ordered Commissioner Horton.

The Bomb Squad carefully, check out the burnt out car before giving the all clear to open signal to the Fire Chief. The crowd of people and reporters gather in the street, but the police manage to push everyone back. "Attention! All citizens! For your safety! Please return to your homes!"

The news agencies expected us to allow them to stay, but they were forced further away by the crowd of people, so they decided to call in the big guns. The television news station immediately sent in a chopper to fly overhead. "They are going to be a problem and I'm going to get rid of this problem," I told Christian.

I unclipped my iPhone from my belt and hit speed dial #1 and immediately a male came onto the line and I said, "I need a favor."

A lot sound is heard from a distance and everyone look up and sees an fully armed Boeing AH-64 Apache quickly approaching the News Chopper. Captain West looks up and sees the Apache, then walks over to me and Christian and say, "Who in the hell sent for the United States Air Force?"

"We don't need photographs of Denishia's body turning up on worldwide news."

Captain West watch's as all the reporters and Satellite News Trucks immediately pack up and leave

The pilot of the Apache asks on his loud speakers to the pilot of the News Chopper, "State your intentions!" The News Chopper pilot saw the Apache and left the crime scene air space without haste, and my iPhone rings and one look at the Caller-ID and I knew who it was. The pilot of the Apache asks, "Should I chase them?"

I looked at Captain West and ask, "The pilot wants to know if you want to chase the News Chopper?"

Captain West looks at me crazy and responds, "Is he crazy?"

I smile and tell the pilot, "No. Thanks for the help."

"Anytime," responded the Apache as he flew off in another direction.

The Fire Chief walks over and tells me, "We'll have the vehicle open shortly."

I tell him, "Fine, just let me know."

Captain West suggests, "We need to look inside her Loft while things are still fresh."

It didn't take long for the Fire Department to pry the door of the car open and the Crime Scene Investigators and the Bomb Squad Team moved in to collecting evidence.

Captain West and I were walking up the back flight of stairs when one of the Investigator calls out to me, "Detective Breeze you need to take a look at this!"

"I'll be there in a minute," I said to Captain West.

"No problem," he said noncommittally.

I walked over to the Denishia's car and stooped down on the driver's side to take a look. If I had worn glasses this would have been the point when I would have pulled them off and begin to nervously chewing one of the earpieces, but instead I held on to my iPhone and gently tipped it on my chin. Christian walks over and stands behind me, "She's has something clinched in her fist."

Medical Examiner, Dr. Hussein arrives and walks up and stands next to Christian.

I stand up, "Yes, but what?"

Dr. Hussein replies, "Give me a few minutes and I will have an answer."

CHAPTER 26

Detective Virginia Breeze

Captain West is standing at the front door, "It was kicked in" Captain West comments to Officer Jenkins.

Virginia walks over still wearing the rubber gloves, and looks at the door, "Did the neighbor's hear anything?"

Officer Kincade walks over interrupting, "You know the story, everyone was home, but no one heard a thing."

"The building manager tried to get us a printout of the various people that used the key card to gain entry, but the computer malfunctioned and the data was not retained-"

Captain West is looking up at all the central of entry and ask, "What about the security videos?"

Officer Kincade interjects, "The recording is missing."

Virginia, "Did someone break in?"

Officer Jenkins looks at Kincade, "If there was, then the building manager didn't file a police report."

A short man in his seventies, on a walker, walks towards Virginia, "You'll need to speak up he's a little hard of hearing," said Officer Kincade.

Virginia asked, "Who in the heck is he?"

Officer Jenkins, "Mr. Thompson, the Building Manager."

Captain West utters skeptically, "You've got to be kidding." as Mr. Thompson comes over.

Mr. Thompson stops his walker in front of Denishia's door, he looks the door backwards and forwards, "Who's going to pay for this?"

"Do you own this building?" asked Captain West.

Mr. Thompson looks up at Captain West, "Heck no, somebody down town owes this."

Captain West, "Really?"

"Whom do you mean?" I ask smiling at him.

Mr. Thompson smiles back at Virginia and motions for me to walk with him to his apartment, and they stop in front of his door, "It's open."

Virginia opens the door, and Mr. Thompson says, "Ladies first."

Virginia walks up and Mr. Thompson enters behind her and closes the door, and as he folds his walker and sits it in recliner in the corner of the room. He points at the brown sofa, "Have a seat and let me talk to you."

Speaking loudly, "Who is the owner of the building?"

"Stop yelling I'm not deaf, "says Mr. Thompson.

She laughs, "I thought you were hard of hearing?"

"I hear what I want to, when I want to," he informs me. Mr. Thompson turns on a breathing machine, and runs the tube around his head and into his nose, "The owner is the Director of the State Gaming Commission."

I gave Mr. Thompson a curious look, "The State Gaming Commission?"

"Yeah, you know the people that run the Lottery."

I said, "These are some nice Lofts."

Mr. Thompson, "A little too upscale for Denishia's salary."

"She paid her own rent?" I ask.

"No she didn't…he paid it like clockwork the first of every month," said Mr. Thompson.

I sat down on the foot stool just in front of Mr. Thompson, "Who was it?"

Mr. Thompson reflects on it for a second, "Well I'm not supposed to discuss it, but since its part of your investigation…well…I guess."

There was a knock on the door, and a female voice calls out from the hallway, "Gramps! Are you in there?" A voice calls from the closed door.

"Oh crap, not her again!" Mr. Thompson points towards the door for Virginia Breeze to open it. I bent closer to Mr. Thompson and asked again, "Who paid her rent?"

The woman cries outs again, "Gramps!"

Mr. Thompson looks at the door then looks at me, "Who paid her rent?"

Again, "Where are you, Gramps?"

Mr. Thompson looks frightened as he glances at the door, and I stood up and ask, "Is there something wrong?"

He nodded his head and answered, "I don't like her."

I tried to console him, "I want let anyone hurt you. Just tell me who paid her Denishia's rent?

"His name is," he was about the tell me when a a woman of about twenty-two years old, with her hair pulled back wearing red jeans with angora sweater and low heels used her keys to enter his apartment.

She hurries to the old man, "Don't say another word Gramps!" The woman pushes past Virginia and hugs Mr. Thompson, "You had me so worried, why didn't you answer your phone?"

Mr. Thompson laughs, "I forgot it and left it on the nightstand."

"You need to keep it with you at all times," she said to Mr. Thompson.

The woman says, "My Grandfather is very sick and not able to answer any more questions."

Mr. Thompson suddenly has a fit of coughing and I offer, "I can call for help?"

The woman has a short irritated dry tone, "No. He needs to catch his breath."

I ask, "May I ask your name?

Mr. Thompson stops coughing and she answers, "Fay Marden."

Mr. Thompson starts coughing and shaking his head, but he finally catches his breath, and he tells me, "Detective Breeze that's all I'm able to tell you at this point, but come back later." Fay gives Mr. Thompson a strange glare and he blanks out, but I believe I caught on to what he was trying to tell me. That was his way of communicating that Fay Marden was not her name.

Virginia heads for the door, "Thank you Mr. Thompson and I'll be in touch if I need anything else." The woman stands in silence as Virginia got ready to leave. I could see a look of fear in his eyes as he watched me leave. I was hoping he would ask for help or something, but nothing.

CHAPTER 27

Captain West

Virginia walks in with her iPhone in hand with a certain kind of arrogance and smugness that would make the most demure exit the room. I ask her, "You get anything useful out of the old guy?"

"A little bite..." she stops mid-sentence when she spots Denisha's computer crushed and smashed on the floor. The first thing we noticed was the untouched Chinese take-out boxes sitting to the right of the shattered computer and looks at it and ask, "What in the world?"

"Hard to tell, but a safe guess is someone was beyond angry," I answered.

"She was working on something, but what?" as Virginia looks at the broken pieces of the computer.

Officer Jenkins walks over carrying an empty box; he starts to carefully place the pieces of the computer in the box. He suggests, "I could have Tom Johnson and the tech guys have a look and see whether or not anything can be retrieved from the hard-drive?"

Virginia purses her lips and glances in Captain West's direction, "I don't think so. That box is coming with me." She stoops down on the floor, "I'll box this up," and she takes the box from Officer Jenkins.

Officer Jenkins stands up in a slight huff, as he and Kincade look at one another hoping for something quick to say, but Captain West's rough, course voice, "What's the problem with you two?"

As Virginia continues picking up the crushed pieces of the computer, and places them delicately into the box, she can hear the hesitation in Kincade's voice, "No problem-it's just that..."

Jenkins rubs his hand through the two-day stubble on his face, "We were thinking Tom and the tech guys could have a look at this stuff and see if they can retrieve some of the data."

Kincade adds, "He's good at this kind of thing."

"I'm sure he is, but we'll let Detective Breeze handle it her way at the moment," I told both men.

"He'll destroy what's on it," whispers Virginia under her breath.

I looked down at Detective Breeze, "Did you say something Detective?"

"I said they have nearly destroy it," she answered.

That didn't sound like what she said, but maybe my ears were playing tricks on me.

Virginia picks up the box, and says, "I'm going to see what progress has been made by the Crime Scene investigators."

Using his large frame, Office Kincade blocks the door in an aggressive stance, "The computer is evidence and know unauthorized personnel are allowed access because it is part of a homicide investigation."

Kincade reaches for the box and I shoved his narrow butt aside and told him, "I call the shots here not you!"

Detective Breeze quickly leaves as Jenkins yells from across the room, "This is the last straw-Internal Affairs is going to hear about this...you big black..."

"Go ahead and say it so I can shove those words so far down your throat you'll be constipated for a week."

Officer Jenkins watches Virginia from the window as she places the box in the trunk of her car and slams the trunk shut.

Kincade and Captain West is standing toe-to-toe and eye to eye, and in a low tone of voice, Kincade says, "It's just a matter of time, but you will be working for me."

"I'll retire first," says Captain West.

"If you make it to retirement," he said with a Machiavellian laugh.

Officer Jenkins gathers up the few bits of remaining evidence, and as he and Kincade turn to leave, Jenkins says, "You can retire now if you want to." Jenkin and Kincade leave.

I shouted out, "When I'm finished with you two you'll be lucky to get a job as a Dog Catcher!" "On second thought…Even the dogs don't deserve you two!"

I was so angry and I almost missed Mr. Thompson when he opens his door and peeps out at me as I was leaving, "That's telling them!"

CHAPTER 28

Detective Virginia Breeze

Even in full Military fatigues and combat boots, Chief of the Bomb Squad, LT. Jack Mangano stands six foot four, and two hundred and fifty pounds and he is holding a small computer chip in large hands flipping various dipswitches. Bomb Squad team member, John Burton hands another small component to Lt. Mangano, and the two chips snap perfectly together. Virginia walks over, and "What'd we know so far?"

Lt. Mangano hands the small computer component to me and I look at it on all four sides, and Lt. Mangano, "The switch is not very sophisticated, but it got the job done."

I asks, "How many people have this capability and know how?"

"Something this simple could be learned from the internet," comments John Burton.

"And the stuff that makes it go boom can be a little harder to come by," said Lt. Mangano ask he takes the component from Virginia.

"If it were me, I'd start with someone that has construction and demolition experience," said Burton.

A tow truck stops and Lt. Mangano gives the driver the signal that it is okay to load it onto the bed. The driver, a thin young man in his twenties wearing greasy overalls and black steel toe boots, waves back to Mangano. He hooks the anchor of the truck to the burned out Jeep, and the Jeep is lifted onto the bed of the truck, and then he jumps back into his truck.

A young man of sixteen wearing baggy sweat pants, and shoulder length dreadlocks runs over with his video phone and takes a picture of the car. I yell at him, "Hey stop!" he takes off running with me with Lt. Mangano in hot pursuit on foot., We run through a narrow passageway of two buildings and the young man runs into a high-rise apartment building. We enter the building and find numerous apartments to the right and left with small children running and playing in the hall. Music from one of the apartments echo's into the hallway. A number of women stand in the door of their individual apartments watching their children at play. Mangano yells, "Which way did he go!"

Silence from everyone, a woman opens her door, "Tweety-Boo, come in here."

Two six-year-old boys are playing tag in the hall; another woman comes out of her apartment, "Lil-J come inside."

The two boys wave to another and the women and children go back into their apartments and close the doors. I must admit I was out of breath and panting and said, "He's in one of these apartments."

"It'll be next to impossible to know which one," said Lt. Mangano.

Finally, catching my breath, "You're right, so let's go."

As they turn to leave, Mangano stops and points at the crayon marks and other graffiti on the walls, "See this, I don't understand any of this."

Virginia stops and looks, "Typical section-8 housing."

"They live where they can afford," I comment.

"I understand that, but why is this building located in a section of the city with Multi-Million Dollar Lofts?"

"I see what you mean, but the next question is how Denishia was able to afford a Loft," asked Virginia.

"Now that's a good question," said Mangano.

As we were leaving one of the door creaked open and the six year old named Lil-J comes out and slowly approach us and says, "Excuse me."

I stopped and smiled at the little guy, "Yes. What can I do for you?"

Lil-J asked, "Did someone hurt Denishia?"

Despite having two small children of my own, I am still unprepared for a question like this from a small child. I said, "Yes."

Lil-J lowered his head in sadness, and I ask him, "Did you know Denishia?"

He looks up at me, "Yes. She used to live here until she moved to a nicer place."

"Oh really, I didn't know that," I said.

"She moved in with her boyfriend Tyrone Lane…he's rich," said Lil-J

Lt. Mangano reaches into the deep pockets of the Military Fatigues and takes out a hand full of candy and gives it to Lil-J. Both of his hands were full of candy, and I said, "Thank you for helping me."

Lil-J's mother comes out into the hallway and screams, "Get into the house Boy!"

Lil'J runs into his apartment and we could hear her fussing at Lil-J, "What did I say about talking and taking candy from strangers?"

CHAPTER 29

Nadine Dalton

Six-year-old Liza is sitting on the couch playing with a doll watching cartoons while her eight-year-old sister Madison is doing her homework with our families pet Cockatiel named Jeremiah sitting on her shoulder. Nadine is busy picking up the living room. Grandma, Nadine Dalton is an elegant woman in her seventies; she looks at the clock on the wall-8 P.M. "Girls, time for bed."
Liza puts on a sad face, and begins to whimper, "Can't we wait for Mommy?"
"She's going to be late again…as usual," Madison blurts.
I attempt to reassure them, "She'll be home soon."
I am no worst the liar today than any other day, but that was all that is required to convince Liza, but Madison was a different matter. Madison packs her books in her book bag, and Liza holds her doll close as she skips off to her room.
Narrowing her eyes, and focusing on the Cockatiel of Madison shoulder, "Put Jeremiah back in his cage."
Madison extends her index finger up to her shoulder and Jeremiah hops onto her finger, and she walks over to his cage sitting on a small table in a corner. She whispers, "Time for all good little birdies to go to bed," as she opens the cage door and sticks her hand in and Jeremiah hops onto his perch and she closes the door. Madison kisses her Grandmother, "Goodnight Grandma."
Nadine looks at Jeremiah's cage, "We'll need to clean his cage tomorrow."

110

Madison looks at the cage, "It doesn't look so bad."

I loathe a dirty house and I don't particularly like the idea of animals in the house, but it wasn't my idea. I am no braver today than any other day, but Jeremiah was a gift from their late father, so I tolerate the bird. Looking over the cage, "It doesn't look that good either." Madison picks up her book bag and goes to her room as I fix my eyes on the coloring book, markers, and toys covering the floor, "Look at this mess."

I continue my nightly ritual of cleaning up before bed each night. There is a sudden crash from the back patio. I walk to the window to investigate and I quiet look out of the window and I see my daughter in law, Virginia with her gun drawn and about to shot the neighbor's German Shepard for turning over the trashcan and ranting,

"You'd better keeping in your yard or you'll have a dead dog."

I shook my head and returned to cleaning the living room floor. I pick up a pink, yellow, then green marker and Virginia unlocks the door while talking on her iPhone, "Let me call you tomorrow-okay-bye." Virginia closes the door and locks the double-sided double cylinder deadbolt lock on the door.

She throws her keys on the mantle of the fireplace, "Hey Mom."

Walking quietly through the hall, Virginia takes off her jacket and hangs it in the hall closet. Nadine, "Hello, your dinner's covered up on the stove."

The baby Grandfather clock in the hallway chimes nine times. Virginia and Nadine walk through the hall into the kitchen and Virginia asks, "Kids in bed?"

I told her, "They've been in bed for about an hour now."

Virginia joked, "They are probably still up and playing."

I said, "Probably."

I keep myself up on all the Local and National News, and I said to Virginia, "I saw that car bombing on the news and that Helicopter guy is mad at you guys."

"He had no business invading our air space," she said as she laughed.

"The news said the victim lived in those expensive lofts and that she was also employed at the Police Department," I told her.

"It was Denishia," Virginia said.

Shocked and surprised, "You mean you assistant?"

"Oh my God," I stated.

I told her, "She a member of our church?"

Virginia replied, "Really?"

"Yes. She the one that was having the affair that a married man...it was quite the scandal," I said.

Virginia asks, "Who was it?"

I know when she's fishing for information, so I told her, "Tyrone Lane."

Virginia and I walk into the kitchen and she picks up the plate. She pulls off the foil from the plate, baked pork chop, streamed vegetables, macaroni and cheese; she sit is the plate in the microwave for three minutes, she walks over to the refrigerator and opens it. She is bent over looking in when she spots it, lemonade.

"I knew that name sounded familiar, but I didn't know exactly where I'd heard it," said Virginia.

I hate gambling. I always have. Virginia father was a professional gambler and I almost though that's what she was going to be after college, but she got involved with the NSA . I told her, "If you went to church more you would know who he is," I stated,

"He's the guy that's head over that lottery."

Virginia tried to change the conversation by asking me, "What else was on the news today?"

"That Billion Dollar Lottery Ticket winner still hasn't come forward," I told her laughing, "I was talking to Beulah the other day and told her too bad that ticket in the collection plate wasn't the winner?"

She grabs the bottle of lemonade from the refrigerator as the microwave beeps, and she walks over to me and demands, "Repeat that!"

The look in her eyes told me she had no idea, "Too bad that Lottery Ticket was a loser."

Virginia continued to glare at me, "You said something about a collection plate?"

"Yes. I found a lottery ticket in last Sunday's collection plate," and "I told Beulah and she said she would destroy it once she got into the counting room," I told her.

Virginia asked me like she was interrogating me, "Who else knew about the ticket?"

I thought carefully and my mind drew a blank, "Just Beulah as far as I know."

Virginia removes the piping hot plate from the microwave.

She made me so nervous I felt drained. I told her, "Goodnight," and walked up the stairs to my room.

Virginia said, "Goodnight. I'm turning in as soon as I eat and check my email."

CHAPTER 30

Detective Virginia Breeze

I love my private library because it has everything I need, my private gun collection and various books about collecting guns and a computer system that allows my full and exclusive assess to any and everything. I decide to walk down the narrow hallway into my private library and check my NSA email while I eat dinner. Opening the bottle of lemonade and takes a drink as I begin going through the various NSA Security Access points. The last screen asks for my username and password. I went directly to the email section and saw a message flashing and arrow directly to the message marked Urgent!!!

The name Denishia Logan popped up on the screen, "Denishia sent this before she was killed."

Virginia begins reading the file regarding Shawn Graves dated 1986:

Inmate: Shawn Graves III was badly burned on his face, and hands. After several months in ICU and reconstructive surgery, Shawn was released from prison.
Original Sentence: 10 years for Felony Drug Possession.

I begin reading a supplementary file. I look at Shawn Graves' mug shot and the original arrest record. It seems the Officer Cornelius West was the arresting officer. As I read, the thought keeps suggesting itself, "This is the explanation for Captain West's intense interests in the Murdock Case." Under the circumstance's it would be best to speak directly to Captain West. I continue reading the account of the prison fire in which Eric Campbell died in June of 1986. There is another file attached. I point the curser and the file opened and it read:

Inmate, Eric Campbell was found dead in his cell at approximately 6:54 A. M. Wednesday, October 1, 1986. Campbell's death is among several unexplained deaths. The Medical Examiner'sConclusion: Dead before the fire.
Current Status: Body Cremated.

I open the photo file attachment. From the moment I looked at the photographs of both men, something stunk to high heaven. Back and forth I continued to flip between Shawn Graves photograph and Eric Campbell's and the two men are almost a dead ringer. I keep staring at Eric Campbell's mug shot and the man bears a shocking resemblance, but it is clearly not the man claiming to be Shawn Graves today, but after extensive plastic surgery, they wouldn't match. I look at the name and, photograph of the Warden in charge of the prison and it was Allen Thompson, "Nuh uhhhhhhh!!!" Upon closer examination, it appeared that the Allen Thompson from the prison and old Mr. Thompson, the apartment loft manager, are one in the same, "Well I'll be doggone."

The sun was bright, and the morning air is humid, thunder rumbles from a distance as Virginia gets out of the car. It is not her usual car, but a loaner from the Police Department. Virginia hates departmental cars because no matter what they do, it still has the look and feel of a police car, and in her opinion, that can make his a moving target in some communities. She parallel parks along the curb in front of the Clarkson Lofts, and she head to the front door, and rings the buzzer. A man with a sleeping voice answers, "Yeah, what is it."

She opens her wallet and holds it up to the camera, "I'm here to see Mr. Allen

Thompson," replies Virginia.

"Doesn't live here anymore," responds the man, then the speaker cuts off.

Ringing the buzzer again, "Now what is it," asked the man in an agitated tone.

"Open up," she demands holding up her badge. The lock opens with a buzz, and he enters.

The guard sits at his desk in the main lobby, Virginia walks over to the desk and he has large box of chicken and a bottle of hot sauce sitting in front of him. The large dark skinned man in a wrinkled gray uniform. His Badge is turned backwards, making it impossible to get his name. He takes a bite out of a plump green jalapeño pepper, "What seems to be the problem?"

"I need to speak with Mr. Allen Thompson," and she starts walking in the direction of Mr. Thompson's apartment. The Guard stands and yells, "I been trying to tell you, he doesn't live here anymore-his daughter put him in a nursing home!"

"A nursing home!" said Virginia.

He takes a bite from a chicken leg, "Yeah, some lady claiming to be his daughter came and got him and said she was putting him in Evergreen Springs on Big Bend Blvd.

"That's interesting…," said Virginia.

"Sure as hell is... he took care of himself and managed this building. I don't buy any of it," he says as he throws his clean chicken bone in the trashcan next to him.

Virginia walks towards the door and leave, and the guard presses the buzzer and the lock release. The guard's phone rings as he watches Virginia go out the door, "Larry here." "A lady cop, looking for information on Thompson, but my bet is she's headed your way.

CHAPTER 31

Detective Virginia Breeze

I felt like a Destroyer crossing the English Channel as I got out of my car and jumped across the obstacle course of water puddles that cover the parking lot of the Evergreen Springs Nursing Home. From the outside, Evergreen Springs has the look of an exclusive retirement community, but nothing could be further from the truth. I haven't been in Evergreen Springs since I was in the NSA and I hid an elderly Italian mobster that was scheduled to testify against a South American Drug Kingpin. Evergreen Springs has all the place would not be a normal person's first choice. After having spoken to Mr. Thompson and reading the files I can imagine his horrification at his daughter bringing him here.

The main entrance has a set of large glass double doors and a mantrap with a reception desk a few feet away. The receptionist is sitting behind a desk that has a number of chairs along the side of her. There is a woman in a blue uniform sitting next to the receptionist and they were engaged in a conversation when I pressed the buzzer. The receptionist presses a button on a white key pad that is attached to the wall. There was a click at the door and I pulled the door open and entered into the mantrap. I pulled the second set of double doors, but it was locked. Thirty seconds later the door clicked open and I walked up to the receptionist and she said, "How may I help you?" The receptionist had the kind of face that hurts to smile and may even cause the roof to collapse. The woman in the blue uniform remained quietly seated next to the reception desk. I showed the receptionist my badge and told her, "I'm here to see Allen Thompson." After the mention of the name, the woman in blue got up and left and a without a word or single gesture and darted into a corner office. The receptionist got up from her desk and went into the same corner office as the previous woman and never returned. I stood there looking around and there were patients walking the halls in a mindless daze.

A moment later, a light complexioned older woman in a gray and black wig with burgundy streaks came out and said with a flicker of apprehension in her eyes, "Good morning, I'm Genevieve Carney," but I knew from the way she shook my hand that the smile was fake and she had no intention of cooperating. It was not a normal hand shake, but a four finger hand shake.

As the old adage goes, if it seems too good to be true, then it probably is would prove more than just an old wives tale. I showed her my badge as she asked, "I'm Detective Breeze and I'm here to see Mr. Allen Thompson."

Genevieve half smiled with her lips scarcely parted and her fingers rose to her lips then she released it doggedly, "This is high irregular." She scowled at me as though I had made an arbitrary request and inquired, "What's this about?"

I smiled thinly, "This is part of a ongoing investigation."

Genevieve shook her head suspiciously, and replied, "I'll take you to him."

I was led down a long corridor and I looked around trying to get a feel of the layout of Evergreen Springs. I could tell from the smell of the fresh paint and new carpeting that it had been recently remodeled. We enter into a large multi-purpose room where a number of patients are either walking on foot or walking in wheelchairs. A small group of patients are sitting in front of a television set watching cartoons and another man is sitting in a wheelchair in front of a glass bird cage watching Finches. It has been slightly more than a day and I almost failed to recognize Mr. Thompson. He looked very frail and confused and Genevieve stopped and patted him on the shoulder, "Mr. Thompson. You have a visitor."

Mr. Thompson turns and looks at Virginia and I look at him. Immediately I knew something was very wrong. I always get a slight twitch in my ear when I know something is out of place and one look at the man in front of me and I knew the problem. I told Genevieve, "I need to speak to Mr. Thompson alone."

"Alright, but I don't think you'll get much out of him," she commented.

"Well I'll be the judge of that," I said.

Genevieve scrutinized me and smiled and begin to walk away, but she stopped short and looked at the clock on the wall, then she turned and walked into a nearby off with a sign on the door, <u>RESTRICTED! DO NOT ENTER!</u>

Mr. Thompson entire demeanor brightened up so much that he looked at me and said, "I thought she would never leave." He smiled and asked, "What can I do for you Detective Breeze?"

"Just out of curiosity," I explained, "What can you tell me about Eric Campbell and Shawn Graves III?"

Mr. Thompson looked around the room and then I looked around the room before he uttered a word. "Eric Campbell and Shawn Graves III were housed in the Trustee's Unit

119

and they shared the same cell. Campbell was doing a time for a double homicide and Graves was due to be paroled the followingday," and he paused and looked around again, "The fire started in their cell and it spread throughout that whole section."

I glanced around the room and noticed a nurse pushing a cart and distributing medications on the other side of the room. Mr. Thompson looked at her and winked and he continued, "Graves and Campbell were so badly burnt if was difficult to know who as who accept by the Number on the shirt of one of them."

We were startled by the sudden slamming of a door. We both turned to look and saw Genevieve coming out of the office carrying a file on her hand she paused and looked at Mr. Thompson. Mr. Thompson was staring at the Finches, but Genevieve turned and walked in the opposite direction. I looked at Mr. Thompson and told him, "Okay. She's gone."

"We had things under control until the Police and that lawyer showed up and created a lot of confusion," he paused.

"What are you getting at," I inquired.

"The number on the dead man's shirt was 102700312 and that was Shawn Graves' number," he sighed, "That was a shame he died like that and the Campbell's shirt was burnt beyond recognition"

Surprised I replied, "That can't be?"

Mr. Thompson smiled at me, "Oh yes it can. By the time I was finished talking to the police and that lawyer it was a ball of confusion between the Paramedics and the Medical Examiner."

Mr. Thompson glanced up at me and sighed intensely, "Let me get this straight. They got the two men mixed up?"

"Yes," he responded, "Eric Campbell and Shawn Graves looked enough alike that they could pass for twins and I think someone switched Shawn Graves' shirt with Eric Campbell's."

"There is still the detail regarding the surgery," I questioned.

Mr. Thompson looked around again to see if the coast was clear before he spoke, "He was paroled while still in the hospital and Shawn Graves' father John had him sent overseas for special treatment."

I commented, "You men cosmetic surgery."

"John S. Graves got sick a couple years later and Eric Campbell came home looking and sounding like Shawn Graves, but I don't believe his mother Mary Graves believe it was her son, Shawn."

I didn't understand, "Shawn Mother?"

"After John Graves died I heard that Mary had lost her mind and Shawn put her into a sanitarium where she died," he replied sadly.

My Thompson looked around and saw Genevieve and a stout security guard walking quickly in our direction. I looked down at Mr. Thompson as he whispered, "That was not my daughter. Get me out of here."

Genevieve walks over with the file in hand, "If you have any further questions, you'll need a warrant!"

Mr. Thompson continued looking at the Finches, and I said, "I will."

Genevieve snaps at the guard, "Will, escort Detective Reed out."

I patted Mr. Thompson on the shoulder, and said, "See you later, and turned to leave with Will following close behind me.

I paused to look back at Mr. Thompson again and he was looking at me with tears in his eyes and I knew that would be the last time I would see him alive. In those final

moments I could hear Genevieve say, "No,
you won't."

CHAPTER 32

The sign read, Inventory Clearance Sale at the auto dealership. Twenty-two year old identical twins, Shatoya and Jade Quinn sit in a Casmir Silver Metallic BMW 6 Series. Jade grips the steering wheel and inhales the smell of fresh Dakota leather, "I want to go for test drive."

Shatoya thought for a hot minute before she spoke, "These folks not let you take this car off the Showroom Floor."

Jade pondered the idea for a moment and said, "I don't see why not."

"Jade," said Shatoya with a crisp reply, "They are going to want to see your Bank Statement plus a Credit Check before they will consider allowing you to test drive this car."

Jade turned to her sister and said, "Ain't no problem they can look at my Bank Statement now if they want to."

Jade continued to stroke the steering wheel as has sister tugged at her wrist and bent over and whispered, "Yeah, but you suppose to have some money on the Bank Statement and money in the bank."

Jade was about to reply, "That's just a…"

But Shatoya stopped her mid-sentence, "Before you say anything else we need to get to work, and she opens the car door and got out.

Jade countered, "We already late," as she gently closes the car door and looks at the sales price on the sticker, "Girl!"

Bolting to the passenger side of the BMW, Jade looks and gets a case of immediate sticker shock, "Jesus will have to pay for it."

"Come on and let's go. Our current salary will never afford any kind of car in the low nineties," said Shatoya as she and Jade walked back to their late model car they refer to as Vicki.

Jade was silent on the drive to work at Spirit Temple Pentecostal Christian Church and Shatoya commented, "We need a better job."

"You would think a well-established church would at lease offer benefits," Jade said quietly.

"Churches are non-for-profit organizations, so if we get laid off we don't even qualify for unemployment," said Shatoya.

Jade reflected on Shatoya's comment for a moment and then said, "God's house sure is a hateful place."

Shatoya and Jade enter the dark sanctuary of the church and Jade flips the light switch on the wall. The floors are decorated with imported hand woven carpeting in navy blue with little black crosses embroidered along the edges. They notice someone sitting on the front pew, surprised Jade said, "Someone is sitting in the dark."

Just as surprised, "What?" said Shatoya. "Hello," said Shatoya, but there was no movement.

As they approached, Jade makes an observation, "That sort of looks like Deacon Murdock from behind."

"Girl stop-you know that man's dead," Shatoya said, never taking her eyes off the man in the front pew.

Shatoya and Jade walked disbelieving and as they draw closer Shatoya said, "What in the Devil?"

They both stop dead in their tracks and looked with stunned horror at Deacon Murdock sitting in the front pew with his eyes wide open and a big grin on his face, wearing a gray suit with matching shoes.

Shatoya cries out, "Shit!" Shatoya turned to leave, but Jade grabbed her arm.

"Wait," yelled Jade, "Look at him," as she pointed to Deacon Murdock.

Shatoya trying to pull herself from Jade's grip, Deacon Murdock is looking at something he is holding in his hand. Jade steps closer to Ray Murdock's body while she pulling Shatoya along with her, "Look at what he's holding in his hand?"

"I don't know and I don't want to know!" said Shatoya, "Let's go," she demanded.

Jade releases her grip on Shatoya as she looks at what in his hand, "Girl look, it's a lottery ticket!"

Shatoya was about to turn to leave, "The one Grandma Vergi been talking about?"

"I can't be certain, but I think so," replies Jade as she looks at the ticket even closer and takes the ticket out of his hand."

"Stop that, you are going to hell…and trying to take me with you…stealing from dead," exclaims Shatoya.

Jade said, "He's not going to need the money, and this ticket will pay cash for that BMW we were just looking at," smiling as she holds the ticket out to Shatoya.

Jade did not offer any token of resistance as she took the ticket and began to investigate it, "And a lot of other stuff," smiles Shatoya.

"See, that's what I'm talking about," as Jade looks around the church, "All we need to do is take the video tape out of the recorder.." said Jade looking directly at Shatoya.

"Yeah, and turn out the lights and leave," smiles Shatoya.

Jade and Shatoya give each other a high five as Jade rushed into the office and grabbed the video tape out of the video recorder. They leave the same way they came in, turning out the lights and carefully wiping down everything they touched.

The Mini speeds down interstate-270, "Slow down!" Shatoya tells Jade.

The speedometer registers eight-five miles an hour, they zoom past the seventy speed limit sign, "We don't have time, we got to get to the lottery office," exclaims Jade.

Shatoya leans forward and looks into the passenger mirror, "I think we're being followed."

"Are you sure-I don't think so," responds Jade as Shatoya turns around in looks out the rear window and spots a black F150 pickup truck with tinted windows hopping from one lane to another to catch up to the Mini.

"That truck is chasing us!" said Shatoya in near hysteria.

Jade responds, "Yeah, I see it!"

The F150 is directly behind the Mini, and Jade looks out her rear view mirror at the F150, "Oh crap-it doesn't have a license plate!" cries, Jade.

The F150 abruptly pulls to the left of the Jade and Shatoya and cuts her off forcing her to turn into Exit-A as the F150 followed close behind. The Mini and the F150 are the only two vehicles on the isolated road that the F150 forced them on, "I told you not to take that ticket!" yelled Jade as the truck rams them from behind shoving the Mini to a guard-rail and down a deep gulley.

CHAPTER 33

Captain West is a talented and determined man, and his chief mission in life is to make police work honorable and respectable. With the loss of his families breadwinner early in life made for a difficult childhood. His paternal grandmother raised him and she emphasized education and hard work. After high school, his worked full-time as a gravedigger, and attended the local community college at night. After college, he took the exam for admittance into the St. Louis Police Academy, and despite the naysayer's he received the highest score, and was accepted. He became a police officer in 1976, and the first lesson he learned, and he had to learn the hard way, "A Devil is a Devil."

Virginia reads over email files, as she places them carefully in a folder, out of the corner of her eye she sees Tom Johnson constantly walking past her cubical every few minutes. Pretending not to notice Tom, she packs her printed pages into a folder and walks to Captain West's office.

Captain West snaps out of his momentary mental sabbatical with a knock on his door, "Come in."

"Got a few minutes?" asks Virginia as she walks in and glances behind her, and notices Tom just outside Captain West's office looking at a clipboard.

Commander West takes a glimpse at Tom in the hall as Virginia closes the door, "Yeah, I needed to speak to you anyway...have seat."

Virginia sits in the chair next to his desk, "What's going on?"

"I have been on the phone all morning, and guess who with?" Captain West was attempting to make every effort to be civil, and Virginia answered, "I have no idea."

"Genevieve Carney at Evergreen Springs and his so called daughter and they were upset because some Government Officials ramrodded their way in and took Allen Thompson," exclaimed Captain West as he open the bottom drawer of his desk and ran his hand down the drawer in search of a something and he pulls out brand new bottle of Scotch and a glass and asked Virginia, "You know anything about it?"

Virginia looked strangely at him and the bottle of Scotch. She looks at the faded and unbroken yellow label and asked, "You still on duty?"

Captain West looks at the bottle, "This was a Christmas gift from fifteen years ago, and I've been saving this for that one case that going to drive me to drinking."

"I was there this morning to ask him a few questions and that was all," Virginia replied.

Now whether or not Captain West knew she was telling a lie or he believed her explanation, Captain West never let on one way or another.

Almost in a whisper, Captain West frowns and leans in closer, "I received an email from Denishia the night of the explosion, and I need some information regarding a case you worked years ago," said Virginia.

He leans back in his seat and scratches his goatee with his thumb, "Watch case? No...let me guess, "Shawn Graves and Eric Campbell?"

Before she could say a word, there is a knock on the door, an all too familiar voice, Tom's, "Tech Services-I need to run diagnostics tests on your computer!"

A whisk of silence, Virginia leans in closer to Captain West, and he bends forward with his elbows on the desk, "What's going on?"

"I'm having problems shaking him…he's been shadowing me since the explosion," as Virginia scoots to the edge of her chair and bended toward Captain West.

The door opens and Tom enters, "I need to do some quick diagnostics on your computer," as Tom walks to Captain West's desk.

"Ah! That's it?" asked Captain West as he opens his lower desk drawer replaces the bottle of Scotch and the glass and takes out a file, then takes out his keys and locks the desk.

In an attempt to make a quick excuse, "There have been some changes in the Software…" responds Tom, but Captain West cut him off mid-sentence.

"Yeah, I don't doubt that," in a nasty crack to send Tom a message.

"Never ending changes." comments Tom.

Captain West looks at Virginia, "Notwithstanding any other problems…we're leaving."

As they walk down the corridor toward the door, "I get the feeling he's dirty," said Virginia.

"Damn that Tom, I don't know whose pulling is strings, but when I do I'm going to ring some necks," snapped Captain West. Suddenly Tom bolts past them in a mad dash, and out the door.

CHAPTER 34

Lisa West and Cornelius West have been married for almost thirty-years. They met freshmen year at Sumner High School, and Cornelius had a big Afro, elevated shoes and brown and orange bellbottoms pants, and her police officer father did not like him at first. Nevertheless, when he realized how smart and ambitious Cornelius was he took him under his wing, and helped pull some strings to help get him into the police academy.

Lisa is in the kitchen watching television, and at precisely twelve o'clock in the afternoon, during the hottest day of the year, the Meteorologist, Gail Danovan on television said, "The current temperature is one hundred and one degrees with a heat index of one hundred and twelve."

Lisa not the best, but she is not the worst either, but she flipped the channel to one of the cooking channels, and she has assembled everything she needs to make Paula Dean's recipe for Chicken Kabob's and Green Onions for dinner.

The kitchen door opens, and Captain West walks in with Virginia following close behind. He walks over and has a look at what is cooking on the grill, "That smells good, we smelled in the driveway," said Cornelius as he gives her a kiss.

"Hey Lisa," said Virginia with a smile.

"I hope he's not working you too hard-" said Lisa with a delightful smile as she slides a piece of chicken and a tomato onto the scourer.

"No more than usual, "responded Virginia.

Cornelius comes up behind her a takes a piece of the chicken from the simmering skillet and sticks the hot chicken into his mouth, "Om, good."

"Be careful it very hot. Lunch is in the refrigerator," said Lisa.

Cornelius walks over to the refrigerator and take out a plate of sandwiches, "Hon, we'll be in my study."

"No problem," smiles Lisa as she continues making chicken kabobs

Captain West looks the television screen and waves, "Bye Paula."

Cornelius enters, bringing a plate sandwiches and cheese, and some strawberries and two bottles of water. "I thought about grabbing the bottle of Cola, but-" looking at the open file folder, he looks at a

mug shots of Shawn Graves, III and Eric Campbell, "Second thought, I should have grabbed the Scotch," said Cornelius.

"That's the file Denisha sent before the explosion," said Virginia.

"I suspected years ago, that something strange was going come up someday," comments Cornelius as he hands Virginia the file from his desk.

As she reads the file, Cornelius removes the plastic wrap from the plate of sandwiches and he

takes a big bite, "There was something strange about that entire case, I remember it as though it were yesterday," he tells Virginia. "It was

my first night on the job, and they used to call us rookies in those days and there were two cops per vehicle. At that time, all rookies started

on the night shift, the night was quiet, and for St. Louis, a quiet night was a blessing," he continued, "My partner, Burt Nelson and I were

returning from a call on 603 Evans-just a routine domestic disturbance, we picked up the guy and drive him ten or so blocks away, then we put him out-just to give him time to cool off, that's off."

"You should have hauled him in and booked him," comment Virginia.

"In those days we weren't allow to interfere between a man and his wife," said Captain West.

"I see," replied Virginia.

Captain West continues telling his story, "Burt drove to one of his favorite speed trap spots to part and hide-even back then we had a ticket quota to make. We'd s there for almost twenty minutes, and suddenly a supped up Dodge Charger flew by like a bullet, right past our speed trap, so we gave chase, and when we pulled the driver over, it turned out to be two teenagers."

Virginia nodded and said, "Shawn Graves and Eric Campbell."

"Yes and when walked up to the car, and as soon as the driver rolled down the window, the stench of the marijuana hit us smack in the face and Eric Campbell pulls a .22 and shots Burt in the head," said Captain West.

Virginia asked, "What happened to Burt?"

"Shawn Graves was about to put a cap in me when his gun jammed and Burt managed to get off one shot at Eric Campbell before he died at the scene…after I cuffed them and searched the car and I found almost three kilos of marijuana in a large trash bag in the trunk," explained Captain West as he continued, "we able to positively identify them as Eric Campbell, but the real shocker, was the son of Elder John S. Graves of Spirit Temple Pentecostal Christian Church, Shawn Graves. The Daddy was well known and respected around the world. Shawn was a minor, and as much as the authorities tried, it was impossible to keep it off the news and out of the newspapers. At that time, St. Louis had two newspapers, and if you know St. Louis, news of Shawn's arrest was already all over St. Louis and the television and newspapers made things worse."

Captain West thought I knew how the court system worked, but by the time the court date rolled around, the stories changed. Shawn Graves cut a deal in exchange for a lighter sentence. By the time, it was over Eric Campbell got life without parole and Shawn Graves got ten years in prison. He said, "However, little did anyone know the real deal?"

Virginia knew he was referring to the fire at the prison and so called mix-up.

"A few years later, rumors begin going around that Shawn Graves was spotted in London, England and He'd had been living there since he got out of the hospital."

Both were hard to identify, but Allen Thompson said he knew by number on the inmates shirt, and Shawn died in the fire and Eric Campbell was able to switch places with him without being detected," he said, but "Every time the Knights of the Black Circle's name come up, things have a way of being swept under the rug…remember that." Captain West takes a drink from his bottle of water, "that's what I know and remember about the incident."

"I think this Eric Campbell issue needs to be settled once and for all," suggest Virginia.

"Uh ah…and we need to get a court order to have the bodies exhumed and get DNA." said Captain West.

"Yeah, that would be the thing, but we may meet with resistance," said Virginia.

Captain West looked at Virginia with a seriousness she's never seen before and she said, "But I don't think we have that kind of time, but we'll burn that bridge when we get to it."

CHAPTER 35

Nichelle is in her car gathering her various reference books and spiral notebooks to take into the church. She gets out of her SUV with her purse on her shoulder and her left arm loaded down with her materials. The quick blow of the SUV horn signals and a thud signals the locking of the doors. She walks towards the front door of the church and unlocks the door, the alarms of the church beeps as she walks over and enters a code to turn off the burglar alarm. A flip of the switch on the wall lights come on.

Nichelle walks towards up the center isle and she notices someone sitting on the front pew, and she calls out, "Good morning and why are you sitting in the dark?"

Silence, as she continues, and she calls out, "Hello!" However, there is no answer, as she gets closer the thought runs through her head perhaps that person is in deep prayer. As she gets closer, she looks and from the back, the person looks faintly familiar, she arrives at the front pew, and suddenly drops everything in her arms on the floor, "Daddy!" She rushes out the way she came with only her purse on her arm, and she bumps into Shawn at the door and nearly knocks him down, but she hits the floor.

While still wearing his black leather driving gloves, he asked, "What's the matter?" He helps Nichelle off the floor.

"Daddy's in the front pew of the church!" cries Nichelle.

"Deacon Murdock is in the front pew of the church…No way that can be…let's go and take a look," said Shawn as he leads Nichelle toward the entryway of the church. He looks and sees someone sitting on the pew as Nichelle pulls herself from his tight gloved grip and runs out the door. Shawn glances back at Nichelle going towards her car and while digging in her purse. Shaw runs to the front of the church and stops dead in his tracks, "This is unbelievable!"

Virginia stoop's down and looks at Ray Murdock sitting on the pew with a big grin on his face, then she stands up to look at him and comments, "Something's off here."
Captain West walks around and examines Ray from various angels in the room, but he sees
nothing wrong, so he sits down on the steps
of the stage. He looks around the room, then
he looks up and sees the camera's and lights.
On the far wall there is an engineering room
with a large window and he sat looking
around and said further, "This place looks
more like a stadium concert auditorium than a
church.
Virginia walks up the staircase and stands at the pulpit and looks directly at Ray Murdock, then it hits her, "I see it!"
Captain West turns around and looks at
Virginia, then turns and looks back at Ray
Murdock, "What? I don't see anything." "Come up here, then have a look," Virginia instructed him.
Without a flicker of hesitation, Captain West gets up and walks up the stairs and stands next to Virginia, and Virginia asks, "You see it?"
Captain's West's eyes widen, and "Oh yeah!" He walks down the stairs and kneels down to look up into Ray's shining porcelain like eyes and the

135

gleaming white teeth. For a moment it looked as though death was staring him in the face, and he stood up in a cold and unnerving sweat.

Virginia looked at him and asked, "Are you okay?"

CHAPTER 36

"Just got case of the creeps," he answered.

Virginia didn't want to seem cold and uncaring, but she had to stay focused and when she knelled down in the same spot and looked up at Ray, but when she saw was something very different. She saw sadness in his eyes that seemed to project into her very soul, but there would be no way for her to console Ray's spirit. "He's looking at something in his hand."

"Captain West jumped at the idea, "Yeah, but what?"

Taking every precaution she responds in a low whisper, "A Lottery Ticket."

He cuts one eye at Virginia, "Say what?"

"A winning lottery ticket was in the collection plate on Easter Sunday," said Virginia.

He shook his head, "Hmm. Who in the devil would do such a thing? That's just crazy," he said ardently.

"What an unbelievable story, but a billion dollars is motivation enough to get any number of people killed," said Virginia.

Captain West suggested, "We've got to burn some midnight oil connecting the dots of the murders," as he stood impatiently watching Virginia.

"Someone came in and discovered the body and took the ticket," he said reluctantly and he paused before continuing, "We're working with a broad spectrum of suspects and a mega church that employs a lot of people."

"A lot of people work her, but there are not that many people on the payroll," commented Virginia.

Captain West looks around again as they allow the Crime Scene Investigator's entry. They exit via the automated turnstiles and the stop to get a close look, "I've never seen a church where you have to pay to get in."

"The system is pretty sophisticated," she said as Captain West started pushing buttons. But nothing happens. She explains, "It's designed to take only debit and credits cards and deduct tithes from each member."

He looks at her in complete shock, "What if you're just visiting?"

"Then the visitor inserts $20.00 into it and then it will allow you to enter," she explained. Captain West joked, "They thought Jesus was mad at the money changers in the temple, heck if he saw this crap he would have send a bolt of lightning to strike these folks dead as a door nail."

Virginia smiled, "Let's pray it doesn't come to that."

They were standing at the entrance when Dr. Hussein walked up to the turnstile carrying his forensics' toolbox. He tried to enter, but the turnstile alarm beeped and Virginia said, "You'll need to use the side entrance and she pointed to her left.

Doctor Hussein looked at the turnstile instructed in a computer automated voice, "Please insert twenty dollars to enter." Dr. Hussein was holding a twenty dollar bill and was about to deposit it when Detective Reed said, "You don't have to pay anything to get into a crime scene."

Dr. Hussein turned and pointed to the older man standing at the door, "He gave me the twenty and said to insert it into the terminal."

"Virginia looked at the man at the door and immediately she knew who it was, "The Junkyard Prophet," she replied.

He turned to smile and wave to her as Dr. Hussein inserted the twenty dollar bill in the turnstile and like magic the terminal responded, "Thank you and May God bless you and multiply your tithe seven fold."

Captain West looked at the electronic turnstile and said, "Now that's too much!"

CHAPTER 37

Dr. Hussein is standing beside the stainless steel examination table holding his clipboard. The form is labeled external autopsy. There is a male figure drawn diagram on the form. Ray Murdock's body is lying in a sitting position on the table. He carefully inspects Ray Murdock's body inch by inch. He starts at the head, he looks at his head and eyes in a downward position, then he looks at the position of his left hand, "Looks as though he's looking down at something he was holding," he tells his lab assistant, Suzanne.

Suzanne has a small electronic measuring device called a Density Gage about the size of a ballpoint pen in her hand and she bends to get a closer look at the left hand, "It's like he was holding something."

Dr. Hussein draws an arrow on the form next to the left hand, and instructs makes note of its position of the head, eyes and hand on his clipboard and he tells her, "See if there is any space between the fingers."

She takes the Density Gage and holds it up close to the area between Ray's thumb and index finger, and a red laser light shoots out between his thumb and index finger and it beeps. She looks at the LED display, "That can't be right?"

Dr. Hussein, "What's the reading," he insists.

Suzanne looks at the reading, "150 gsm."

"Let me take a look," and she hands the Density Gage over to Dr. Hussein and he asks her, "Hold my clipboard for a second?"

Suzanne takes the clipboard as Dr. Hussein carefully does another reading and the Density Gage, "Its correct 150 gsm"

Suzanne asks, "What is a gsm?"

"It stands for Grams Per Square Meter and its only used to measure the thickness of paper," he answered.

Suzanne smiles, "So he was holding a piece of paper?"

"It would seem so. Make note of 150 gsm on the chart," he instructed. Dr. Hussein begins inspecting the neck area in search of the embalming incision, but there is none, "That's strange," he said.

Suzanne watch's closely and asks, "What is it?"

"This man has not been embalmed," he said.

"The police reports indicated that the body was stolen before the undertaker could embalm the body," she said.

"We'll need to get his clothes off," said Dr. Hussein. Suzanne hands him the scissors and he begins cutting his clothing in a straight-line beginning at the right pant leg, and Suzanne begins at the left pant leg. Dr. Hussein cuts the jacket and shirt straight up the middle, and he stops and looks in complete astonishment. Suzanne walks over to the other side of the table, and she freezes and looks at a large black circle branded in the middle of his chest. In the center of the black circle is a small red dot. Suzanne, asks, "What does it mean?"

Suzanne removes a small remote controlled for the overhead camera to take pictures. The camera flashes after each picture and displays it on the viewing monitor. Dr. Hussein replies, "I'm not sure, but Detective Breeze needs to take a look at this."

Dr. Hussein takes off his gloves and surgical gown and walks to his office and Suzanne's iPhone rings, "Hello."

Suzanna, "Girl you're not going to believe what we just found on Deacon Murdock's body?

CHAPTER 38

Lorenenzo's is the best Northern Italian Restaurant in Saint Louis, and they are well known for having best Chicken Marsala because it's made with a tender chicken breast, sautéed with fresh mushrooms, onions and green peppers in a homemade Marsala wine sauce in Region, and it is Kristen and Tyrone Lane's favorite. Tyrone made the reservation two days ago, so Kristen has been looking forward to this night. She and Tyrone rarely get anytime alone since the birth of their son, Derrick a year ago.

Kristen walks in cultured and sophisticated wearing, Giambattista Valli Metallic Brocade Pumps with a black cocktail dress as soon as she entered the maître d' acknowledged her, "Good evening Mrs. Lane, you look lovely this evening."

"Thank you Antonio," said Kirsten as the maître d' escorts her to her table, all the men's eyes were on her, and the women slashed her with switchblade glances of scorn and envy. "Your waiter will be over in a minute," then he pulls out her chair and helps her to sit down, then he walks away.

Tyrone is supposed to meet her at eight sharp, Kirsten checks the time on her iPhone, and it's eight-thirty, "This is not like him," she says to herself. She picks up her cell phone, and begins entering a text message, "I'm at the restaurant, where are you?"

A young and attractive Italian waiter with dark hair and dark eyes, and built like a tennis player of about twenty-two, wearing a classy black tuxedo uniform walks over and introduces and said, "My name is Giuseppe, would you like something while you wait for Mr. Lane?"

Kristen thinks for a moment, she considers herself somewhat of a wine aficionado and she answers, "I'll have a Sassicaia," she tells him as she could feel him dressing her down with his eyes.

Giuseppe smiles at her "Would be my pleasure," he responds.

Her cell phone rings, she looks at the Caller ID, and does not immediately recognize the number, "This is Kristen."

A panicked, fast talking voice, "Mrs. Lane this is Julia, and the police are here and they found Mr. Lane's car with bullet holes in an alley!"

Giuseppe walks over and sits the glass of wine on the table as Kirsten picks up her small clutch purse and walks quickly out of the dining room in quick steps. She exit's the restaurant, and hands the valet her parking ticket, and she says to Julia, "Calm down, I'm on my way home."

Kirsten squalls her breaks as the Mercedes Benz takes the hairpin turn of the circle driveway, and comes to a complete stop behind a Saint Louis Police Department Patrol car.

She quickly gets out of the car, and makes a mad dash into the Lane

Mansion, she finds two uniform police officers in her living room. Julia is sitting on the sofa holding a crying Derrick, "I want Mommy!"

She'll be hear soon," said Julia, trying to console Derrick, and Kirsten enters the room in tears.

"What's going on?" cries Kirsten as Derrick runs and jumps into her arms.

Kirsten looks at his badge, Kincade as he said, "We found your husband's car in South Saint Louis, and it was covered with bullet holes, said Kincade.

The other Officer, Jenkins asked, "When was the last time you saw your husband?"

"This morning before he left for work," sobbed Kirsten as she holds Derrick tightly in her arms.

Officer Kincade looks at Kirsten's appearance and asks, "May I ask where you were?"

"Tyrone was supposed to meet me at Lorenenzo's at eight, and he never showed up," said Kirsten, "then I received Julia's phone call, and I rushed home."

Officer Jenkins, "Although we haven't found his body, but we have reason to believe he may have met with foul play."

"You said there were bullet holes in his car?" asked Kirsten.

"Yes, but there was also blood everywhere," stated Jenkins.

Officer Kincade is writing in a small notepad nonstop, but he pauses as asks, "Did your husband have any enemies?"

"Yes, no, in his line of work...I can't be sure," said Kirsten.

The officers look at one another, and Officer Jenkins asks her, "What does your husband do for a living?"

Kirsten reluctantly responds, "Tyrone is Director of the State Gaming Commission."

"Do you mean the Riverboat Casinos?"

"And the State Lottery," Kirsten halfheartedly responds.

Cold and rude, Officer Jenkins, "Detective Virginia Breeze will be in contact, so don't leave town."

CHAPTER 39

Nadine Dalton

Spirit Temple Pentecostal Christian Church is always crowded, but tonight's service is outrageously crowded and spilling out onto the church lawn, and down the street for the funeral services of Deacon Ray Murdock.

Everyone gathered into the church when Nichelle and Mother Beulah enter the sanctuary. The pallbearers entered, carrying steel brown coffin of Ray Murdock. According to Nichelle all the pallbearers came from Murdock Construction.

A second Hurst pulls up outside Spirit Temple Pentecostal Christian Church carrying the remains of Jean Newton.

A lot of funerals and burial are held on Saturdays in St. Louis, and finally they get around to having the funeral of Ray Murdock and of course, Jean Newton. Some and I don't know who, but it was decided that both funerals should be held jointly. Now that's not a bad thing, but they weren't married. Let me correct that, they were married, but not to one another.

The second issue I have regarding today is of all the people that could do the eulogy of Ray Murdock, why on earth was The Junkyard Prophet chosen and why does his wife, Sister Lady Soul has to sing at every church service and funeral.

Junkyard starts slowly in a low voice, "Deacon Raymond Murdock was a well-respected businessman, and greatly admired pillar of the community, but we knew him as an unfaithful husband," said Junkyard.

The Pallbearers slowly carried in the casket of Raymond Murdock. Directly behind The Junkyard Prophet is a large screen monitor, on the screen is a full body shoot of him as he continues, "His floozy followed him to the grave."

Someone yelled from the back of the church, "Amen!"

Reverend Shawn Graves sat in a Pastor's that is more ornaments than the throne of England, but remain quiet as throughout the eulogy. I've heard a lot of eulogies, but this one takes the cake, the pie and the entire dessert tray.

"I can't say he didn't have any enemies, and can't say he didn't step on anyone," said Junkyard as the pallbearers sat the coffin on the stage. The band is playing a slow instrumental spiritual, and the choir rises she sings one of those tunes that repeats the same one verse lyric repeatedly, "The kingdom of heaven is on earth."

Sister Lady Soul sings the lead, "The Deacon is dead!"

The choir sings, "Amen!"

They must have sung for ten minutes while everyone stood and with each, Amen from the choir, someone managed to get the Holy Ghost, and The Junkyard Prophet looked at the the woman and said, "May as well have a party ladies," and they fainted on the floor.

Reverend Graves looks over at his wife Nichelle and her mother, Beulah, and not one teardrop from them, or anyone in for that matter, but that expected. All his business competitors hated Ray Murdock, and there was still plenty of bitterness over Ray's kicking Mother Beulah out of her own house and moving in Jean Newton.

Junkyard Prophet said, "I'd like to invite the undertaker, Brad Mosley to come up and open the casket, and the Ushers, please come forward."

The Undertaker, Brad Mosley and his son, Troy are wearing a dark suits. Brad quietly walks over to the coffin reaches into his pocket, takes out a long S-Shaped key, walks around to the foot of the casket, inserts the key, and begins turning the key. Brad opens the coffin in shock, then quickly closes the lid of the coffin.

Junkyard looks over at Brad Mosley, "Mr. Mosley?" Brad Mosley motions for Reverend Graves and The Junkyard Prophet.

Both men walked over to the Undertaker, "We've got a problem," whispers Brad, "We need to call the police," said Brad.

Reverend Graves reaches over, and begins to open the top of the coffin. The camera zooms in for a close-up shot on the monitor. When he opens the coffin, it was not the remains of Ray Murdock, but Tyrone Lane.

In the front pew is Mother Beulah, Nichelle Graves, and Spiritualist, Vergi Quinn. Vergi's sister Magda hit a sour note on the pipe organ, and the mood changed in the church. "That's not Ray!" Mother Beulah proclaims in a loud tone.

Reverend Graves walks to the pulpit, and picks up his bible and throws it in the direction of the casket, "I can't believe this."
The Junkyard Prophet looked down and said, "I think the Devil's trying to tell us something!"
A voice yells, "Amen!

CHAPTER 40

Detective Virginia Breeze

I cross a bridge into the interior of the hospital, and as I walk across the bridge I am greeted warmly by a kiss from the sun and a full view of the landscape in front of the hospital. I can see Forest Park and people playing tennis in the double tennis court across the street and the cars entering and exiting the parking garage sitting directly in front of the hospital. Upon entering the main lobby of the hospital, I was swept away by the various curves and vertical shapes that created a swaying affect that would produce light-headedness in some people. Another part of the large lobby is painted in earth and ocean tones and the enormous fountain that sat in the center of the lobby hummed its own unique and peaceful lullaby.

The Information and Concierge Services Desk is located in next to the large glass display window of the gift shop. There are various gift baskets of food and flowers, but it was the gorgeous pink roses and snow white lilies arraignments that stole the show. I paused for a moment of thought about my mother-in-law, Nadine and everything she does for me and the girls, and that I would stop and pick her up some flowers before I leave the hospital. I walked up to the desk and was greeted by the receptionist with shoulder length blond hair and with blue eyes as deep as the ocean and delicate southern drawl that sounds like a throwback from the days of Gone With The Wind, "Good morning. May I help you?"

I showed her my badge and replied, "What floor is the ICU on?"

She smiled politely and asked, "We have ten ICU's here, but if you could give me the patient's name I'd be happy to look it up for you."

"I'm looking for two patients, Shatoya and Jade Quinn," I added.

It only took the receptionist a few quick keystrokes to find who I needed. She jotted the information on a small piece of paper and handed it to me and point in the direction of the elevators, "Take the North Elevator up to the second floor ICU and the Nurse's Station can help you from there."

I smiled and replied, "Thank you."

The Receptionist cheerfully said, "Have a good day Detective Breeze!"

As I and a crowd of people boarded the North Elevator, I remembered quickly flashing my badge at the Receptionist and I figured it was too fast for her to have caught my name, but she had nevertheless, but I suppose it comes with her job.

The elevator arrived at the second floor and I stepped off directly in front of the Nurse's Station and a female spoke in a smoky, fatigued, ICU-weary voice, "Who are here to see Detective?"

From that moment I knew she was the type that my badge would not carry any clout with this Drill Sargent of a charge nurse. I flipped my badge and responded, "Shatoya and Jade Quinn."

"They are heavily medicated and can't talk right now, so you'll have to come back," she said as she got up from the desk and scanned her identification badge along the electronic panel on the wall, then walks a set of double doors and the doors automatically closed behind her. I passed a waiting room as I approached the electronic double doors. I made up my mind to enter at the next opening. I could see through the small window that the Nurse was sitting at another station just into the entryway looking at a computer monitor. She glanced up at me and continued gazing without blinking at the computer screen. I was standing in front of the door when a woman came out of the waiting room and asked, "You here to see my Grand Daughters?"

I looked at the woman and her face seemed familiar, but I couldn't place where I knew her from. I took out my badge and showed it to her, and she responded, "You don't need to show me that Virginia, I know who you are, but it looks like you don't recognize me. I'm Prophetess Vergi Quinn."

I said, "Oh course, I'm so sorry." Of course I remember her now. She used to be a Gypsy Fortune Teller back in the day, and after she had spiritual epiphany in 1959 while riding on the old Hodiamont Streetcar Line in St. Louis and claimed Jesus appeared to her. She is still a Fortune Teller, but she works strictly within the church and she is referred to as Divine Prophetess Quinn.

"I can get you in for a few minutes," She explained, "They have been in and out since they came in, but I wished I knew what

happened," she said looking directly at me.
The Nurse enters the waiting room, "Mrs.
Quinn you may go in for a few minutes."
Divine Prophetess Quinn got up and
motioned for me to follow, but the nurse
stopped us and said, "Only Family."
"She is family," said Devine Prophetess
Quinn.
I wasn't prepared for her to lie, but in is in no
matter how you get in.
The Nurse give me a dirty look, "You might
have said so in the beginning Detective and
saved yourself a lot of trouble." The
electronic doors opened and we entered
following the Nurse, "Come this way," she
instructed. We were led to room 2B and the
Nurse explained, "Jade is still on life support
and Shatoya has some consciousness."
I bent over the side of the rail and took
Shatoya's hand and asked, "I need to find out
what happened to you and your sister?"
Shatoya is off the ventilator, but she is
struggling to take a breath, "I've seen your
name on the membership list."
"Yes, when I have time" I said and smiled.
The Nurse is standing nearby takes vitals for
Jade in the next bed and she turned to me and
said, "Keep it short."
Still holding Shatoya hand I asked again,
"What happened?"
"Jade tried to warn me, but I wouldn't listen
and took it anyway," said Shatoya.
Shatoya's Grandmother asked, "Take what?"
I told her, "Take your time." I tried to get bits
and pieces of information and she tried to tell
me.

"We took the Lottery Ticket from Ray Murdock," she said.

Her Grandmother in shock, "You two stole from a dead man."

Shatoya starts coughing and the Nurse comes over, "It's time for you to leave."

I released her hand and her Grandmother took her hand, "Grandma...it's cursed."

There was a sudden loud pitch beeping sound followed by alarms and teams of people rushing in and pushed Divine Prophetess Quinn and I out into the hall. I remained with her until Reverend Shawn Graves arrived. Vergi was surprised to see Shawn, "I thought Junkyard was coming over?"

"The insurance company finally sent in all the paperwork for Jade and Shatoya's car and Junkyard had to go pick the car up at the police tow yard," said Reverend Graves, "But, he'll be her."

Shawn was caught off guard at my presence and he kept looking at me looking at him. I thought it rather odd that he would be wearing leather driving gloves on such a warm day as this. The current temperature is almost ninety-two with a heat index of one hundred and two degrees. Shawn rubbed his nose with his index finger and said, "I don't think either of the girls are in any condition to talk to you right now Detective Breeze."

Vergi never let on that I had already spoken to Shatoya and neither did I, and we left it at that. I looked at Shawn Graves closely and tried to discern whether or not the man that stood before me was Shawn Graves or Eric Campbell and that is when it hit me. How could I have missed it and it was in front of me the entire time.

Divine Prophetess Quinn looked at Shawn and said, "Thank you for coming."

"I wouldn't leave you here alone. Nichelle should be here soon," he told her.

Shawn sat down in the chair next to Divine Prophetess Quinn and she looks at him and asks, "Aren't your hands hot in those leather gloves?"

He looks at her and said, "These are my hospital gloves…I don't want to catch anything."

I thought Vergi bought his explanation, but I guess she didn't, "It's over a hundred outside and it's too hot for any kind of gloves," and in an attempt to keep her mind off of the twins she continues looking at his hands and the gloves, "I know you're self-conscious about the burns on your hands, but you're among friends."

I stuck around to see whether or not he would remove his gloves, but his wife, Nichelle came in and interrupted and hugged Vergi, "I'm so sorry," said Nichelle. Shawn never took them off, so I quietly excused myself.

CHAPTER 41

Detective West was outside puking up his guts when I drove up, but he managed to get his stomach in working order long enough to streaming out orders like a Drill Sargent, "Put on your Forensic Protection suits now!"

I made no reply and grabbed a suit from a nearby technician and went into the church. The stench hit me like a line drive and went through the Forensic Protection suit like it was being controlled some special stench guidance system. The stench penetrated through the mask and flew straight up my nostrils as I walked as I walked toward the open casket. The team used this as an opportunity to stand back so they could get a breath of fresh air while I took a good look inside at Tyrone Lane and the dense globs of blood that stained the interior of the coffin.

For once, I decided this would be a good opportunity to stay out of the action and allow the Forensics Team to do their job. I exited the church and snatched the head gear and mask from my face and flung it to the ground and coughed as I tried to catch my breath. My lungs felt like a great battle was being waged between the stench and the fresh air.

The entire church congregation was waiting and watching from the North side of the parking lot. I saw everyone, even my Mother-in-law, Nadine. The only missing persons were Shawn and Nichelle Grave and

Kristen Lane. Detective West approaches me and asks, "You okay?"

"Yeah, just needed to catch my breath," I said.

I continued standing there watching the church congregation mingle as though they are at a dinner party. The Undertaker, Brad Mosley and Junkyard Prophet are in a heated discussion, and Brad Mosley gets directly in Junkyard Prophet's face and the congregation gathers around them like school children watching a fight. "We'd better get over there," I told Captain West.

Captain West used the power of his weight to push his way through to the center of the crowd, "Alright! Break it up!"

Brad Mosley turned a deaf ear to me and Detective West and he grabbed Junkyard Prophet by the collar with one his right hand, "Listen here you Jackleg, self-appointed, internet ordained, Son-of-a..."

Brad was about to connect a left hook at the Junkyard Prophet, but Captain West forcefully jerked Brad off of the Junkyard Prophet. Detective West demanded in a loud stern voice, "Stop it now!"

Junkyard Prophet looked relieved to be out of Brad Mosley's Goliath hands and he didn't want to admit that he was scared to death and cracked his trademark charismatic smile and said to Detective Reed, "I'm glad you came over and pulled my off him," he joked and the crowd laughed.

Troy walked over to his father and Brad looked at him, "Everything's fine."

I stood next to Brad and asked, "How in the hell did this happen."

Brad was about to get angry again and said, "Look! Someone is targeting my mortuary for some purpose I don't understand!"

I raised my hands and said, "Lower you voice and calm down."

There was no point in questioning Troy because I know he lives the life of a playboy and the funeral business is the least of his interests. I looked Brad directly in the eyes and demanded, "Where is the body of Ray Murdock?"

Troy answered, "He was in the coffin!"

Captain West walks over and looks at Troy and asks, "What in hell going on now?"

Troy looked sidelong at Captain West and answers, "Doggoned if I know...Deacon Murdock done did a Lazarus number again."

Brad looks at Troy and holds down his head with embarrassment and Captain West shifted his weight from one foot to the other and said, "Sounds reasonable enough for me at the moment."

Commander Keel, Chief of Forensics pulls me to one side and we walked to his Mobil Crime Lab Van and handed me a plastic bag containing a box of .22 caliber bullets. Commander Keel, "We found it in the coffin."

I shook the package and I could hear the raddle of bullets and the box was old and faded from age and there are no scan bars on the package. Captain West walks over and takes the box and all he needed was one quick look, "These fit what used to be called a Saturday night special."

He hands me a second bag containing a single .22 caliber bullet and he explained, "Dr.

159

Hussein just fished it out of the victim's palm and he thinks there are somewhere between fifteen to twenty bullets in the body."

"It's small and easy to conceal," I suggested.

Captain West added, "Saturday night specials only took six bullets at a time."

"The shooter reloaded and continued shooting him," I surmised, "Sounds like someone was very angry," I said looking at Captain West. "Perhaps I need to question his wife, Kristen."

Captain West and I walked across the parking lot and to our respective unmarked police cars, "I got your back."

"Sounds good," I said as I got into my car. Detective West and the two police cars tailgated the entire trip to Kristen Lane's house. I thought: Ray Murdock was a well-known Deacon of the church and it's not unusual to see a packed church. Nadine and some of her church friends are full participants in the Grapevine Doctrine. Nadine told me months ago there someone claimed that Nichelle and Tyrone had been sneaking around, and that there would be trouble if Kristen ever found out. I remember a girl named, Drew that was asked never to return to Spirit Temple Pentecostal Christian Church because she was going out with one of the members that was wealthy and married. Mother Beulah and the Devine Prophetess Quinn took her to the side and told her she needed to find another church and since Drew never tithed more than a dollar, the male members would be better off without her.

The 10,000-square foot Lane Mansion sits perched on top of a hill within the wealthy, gated, cul-de-sac community in the historic community of St. Charles. Murdock Construction completed the new expansion that included a split-level, four-car garage and a car elevator.

Our marked police cars and the unmarked from the City of St. Louis dominated the circle drive, but it came as no surprise when the St. Charles police decided to join in. Everyone got out of their respective unit and Captain West commented, "Who sent for them?"

One of the Officers was about six-feet five and his tight fitting uniform made him look skinny and his size sixteen shoes him walk with an unbalanced rhythm, I said, "I hope he doesn't trip and fall."

The other Police Officer remained silent and I've seen his type before. Quiet, reserved and when he does speak it is something worth paying attention to, and I almost forgot to mention, make him angry and he'll put you in your grave.

I rang the doorbell and Kristen's household Manager Slash Personal Assistant came to the door. The woman in her early thirties with light brown hair and while the woman seemed surprised, I thought she must have momentarily forgotten English and reverted back to her native Scottish Gaelic tongue, "Feasgar math."

Both I and Captain West flashed our badges, and I responded, "Good Afternoon."

Captain West asks, "Do you speak English?"

She looked at him with a blank expression and said, "Tha, beagan."

I can hear the St. Charles Police Officers snickering under their breath, and I looked at her and smiled, "Chan eil aon chànan gu leòr." The scoffing ended when she responded to me in clear English, "I guess one language is never enough."

"Sometimes it's more than enough, but I need to speak to Mrs. Kristen Lane."

She reverted back to Gaelic and instructed us, "Tromhadaibh," and she lead us through to a set of elevators and said in English, "Mrs. Lane is in the garage."

We boarded the elevator and I said, "Tapadh leat," but she stayed behind. I looked at the key pad and there was only one way to go, "Straight up." I saw her walk away as the door closed.

One of the uniformed officers looked at me and said, "I used to be a City Cop and I know they don't teach Scottish Gaelic at the St. Louis Police Academy-Who are you?"

I never said a word, but Captain West looks back at both men and said, "Stay out of this."

The Officer made every attempt to explain himself, "I just wanted to know. It's not a common language around St. Louis or St. Charles."

I asked, "Your family Gaelic?"

"My father-in-law," responded the tall police officer.

The quiet officer stopped and looked back at the elevator and commented, "The foreign woman must be new here."

Detective West and I looked at one another, but made no comment as the elevator door opened into a four car garage and we stepped off in front of a classic candy apple red, 1965 Ford Mustang. We looked around and didn't see anyone, but there is an engine running. We kept walking until we saw someone sitting in a white 1962 Ford Mustang Roadster. I tilled my head to one side and looked it was Kristen Lane slumped over in the car. I took off running with Captain West right behind me, and I said, "No,no,no!"

I tried to open the door, but the Mustang was locked from the inside, and the quiet policeman walks over with his night stick in hand, "Stand back!"

He swung his nightstick like Japanese Samurai warrior and I could hear the nightstick slashing the air like a Wakizashi Sword. It tried to shield my face from the flying shards of glass from the shattered passenger window. We began coughing from the sudden release of fumes from the interior of the Ford Mustang. The o

fficer reaches his long arm into the car and shuts off the engine. Detective West and I walk around the car and look underneath and discovered a russet potato rammed up the tailpipe.

The tall officer unlocks the car door and opens it and he knew as did everyone present, Kristen Lane is dead. I stood there looking at the empty backseat then I looked at the passenger side of the car and saw a note. I pulled a tissue from my pocket and unfolded the note, "It's a suicide note."

The elevator door opened and I heard a woman's voice calling out, "Anyone in here?"

I was still holding the note when I yelled, "Police!"

As she was walking over, I recognized her from the first night came to inform Kristen about the blood and bullet holes in her husband's car. I believe her name is, "Julia."

The tall officer yelled, "Don't come any closer!"

Julia kept asking over and over again, "How did you get in here?" and "Where is Mrs. Lane?" Captain West is so robust that he was able to block Julia's view of Kristen's body. Captain West motioned for one of the officers to go over and keep Julia calm, the smaller of the two officers said, "I know her, I'll do it. He rushes to Julia, and she called his name, "Dave! The taller of the two officers stood a little further away taking on his radio and Captain West is on his iPhone in another corner of the garage. Within a few minutes I heard sirens from a distance. I looked at the suicide note: I've finished killing Tyrone and now I have overstayed my welcome. I enjoyed being rich and pretty. Kristen Lane.

Police Officers from St. Louis City and St. Louis County crowed into the parking garage. I placed the note back on the seat of the Ford Mustang.

I walked over to Captain West and said, "I'm going downstairs to talk to Julia," and he followed me onto the elevator. The elevator stopped on the main floor adjacent to the living room, and I found Julia sitting on the sofa in tears. I could tell that Officer Dave had told her about Kristen.

Officer Dave informed me, "This is Mrs. Lane's cousin Julia Nichols."

"I'm sorry for your lost, but I need to talk to Mrs. Lane's Assistant," I said.

"She does not have a personal assistant-just me," she said.

"The foreign lady that just started working here," said Officer Dave.

Julia looked at me and said in no uncertain terms, "There are no foreigners that work on the Lane Estate."

The tall officer walks over and hands me the suicide note and it was in a plastic evidence bag. I read the note again and Julia asked, "What is it?"

I showed it to Julia and immediately she said, "This not Kristen's handwriting."

"Are you sure?"

"Of course, I can get some of Kristen's canceled checks to prove it," said Julia.

Captain West asked Julia, "Do you have any idea why she would do this," he asked.

Julia thought long and hard for a split second, "She caught Tyrone with another woman."

I asked, "Who was it?"

"Nichelle Graves," answered Julia.

I asked, "You sure about that?"

"As a matter of fact she said the Nichelle's daughter, Jenna is Tyrone's," she said.

CHAPTER 42

Detective Virginia Breeze

I tried to get some sleep, but my mind kept hitting the auto-play of the events of the last few days. Just as I about to drift off to sleep, my minds needle got stuck on Sunday. My mind went over a list of things to do: One, prove Shawn Graves is really Eric Campbell. Captain West and I decided to keep Kristen Lane's suicide note under wraps for the time being. It is one thing to have theory as who the killer could be, but proving it can be something different all together. My subconscious just flipped the auto-play fast forward in time. The second most important element on that to-do-list, smoke out the killer of Ray Murdock. I floated from here to dreamland and paradise as my mind concocted the perfect dish to bring the sadistic maniac out into the open.

The ringing of the iPhone awakened me from a deep slumber. I checked the clock: Six-fifteen Saturday morning. It was Captain West, "Have you ever heard of A.C. Automotive?"

"No," I answered, still feeling tired sleepy.

"It's a subsidiary of Carney Steel Industries, Inc."

The name Carney hit me like sledgehammer, "Alvin Carney a.k.a The Junkyard Prophet."

"That's him...I need for you to go back out there and search Shatoya and Jade's car again."

"Not much left of it, but I'll do it."

"I need to warn you...Carney, the businessman is a ruthless cutthroat, so watch yourself," said Captain West.

"I will," I said nonchalantly.

"A FedEx package arrived for you a couple of days ago, but if you came into the office more often you wouldn't need to be reminded," he said sarcastically.

I arrived at A.C. Automotive at eight this morning. I showed my badge to the receptionist at the desk and she quickly directed to follow the arrows that are marked on the floor to the salvage yard. As soon as I walked into the salvage yard the scent of motor oil and axel grease hit my nose and I felt as though I had just stepped into a car cemetery. It only took to whiff before I realized the oil, grease and gas is where the cars life comes from. Tossed carelessly to the ground is a mournful teardrop headlight from a 1959 Chevy. This was the first time I have ever been to an auto-salvage yard, and this looks to be the size of four football fields and all the cars are lined up neatly in roles that seem to go on for miles. I notice small wooden crosses planted on the driver's side of the ground and other cross has staked its claim in the gas tank of a 1962 Oldsmobile Dynamic.

"Hello sweetie, and let me welcome you to my automotive boneyard!"

Startled, I quickly turned around and saw Junkyard Prophet standing behind me wearing greasy overalls and he was carrying battered Hollander Manual that looked like it had been one to many rounds and was now TKO, "Good morning," I said with a smile.

He smiled as asked, "What can I do for you today?"

I answered, "I need to take a look at Jade and Shatoya's car."

"No problem. Follow me," Junkyard said.

Junkyard walks quickly and I tried to have a friendly conversation, "How on earth did you end up in the auto-recycling business?"

"My father was an auto mechanic, so when he needed a certain part he'd come here and we would walk, kick tires and search for the make and model until he found it," he continues, "When I got older, the owner, Peter Richardson give me a job after school and on Saturdays and he taught me everything he knew about the auto salvage business, and when he died, he left it to me," he said.

Just out of pure curiosity, or just know you don't get something for nothing, "Wow. Didn't his family have something to say about leaving this business to an employee?"

"Not really...he had no family as far as anyone was concerned," he answered, "A lawyer from the church handled his entire estate, and let me tell you something," he stopped and went silent for a moment as he looked around as though he was lost in a cemetery.

I asked, "What is it?"

"Mr. Richardson told me more times than I can count that I needed something I could fall back on once and my dad were gone and working for other people was the best way to be poor and stay poor, so he left me this salvage yard, but I had to rebuild it and expand on it," Junkyard explained.

"This is it," I commented.

Junkyard laughed, "This is only part of it," he continued to explain as we continued our long hike through the salvage yard.

We finally arrived at a fenced in area with numerous car that what you could considered totaled, "Why is this separate from the rest?" He said, "These are still waiting for the auto insurance company to release the death certificate on all these, then I can move them to the other area."

I laughed, "You mean the title?"

He laughs, "Yeah. Insurance companies can be a little slow on this sort of thing."

"I bet," I answered.

Junkyard commented, "You guys already search it and released it to me."

I walked around and looked at the late model Ford Crown Victoria and it looks like it had been beaten severely by King Kong. The roof is smashed in, part of the front end is almost twisted, "This is unbelievable." The passenger door and part of the back door had been cut and all the seats had been removed.

I stuck my head in to look around and I failed to notice Junkyard when he walked around to the driver's side and stuck his head in, "Jade and Shatoya are lucky to be alive," he commented as I climbed into the car with a hope against hope of finding the ticket.

"Sure are," he said as he props one foot on the edge of the car and leans over and looks at me and says, "That ticket not in here."

I stopped dead in my tracks, afraid that I didn't know Junkyard Prophet as well as I thought I did and that he may have gotten the drop on me and I attempt to play it off, "What ticket?"

Junkiyard Prophet burst out laughing, "Hahaha…you know what ticket I'm talking about," he said and continued, "Everybody in St. Louis has heard about that ticket showing up in the collection plate Easter Sunday."

I climbed out, "What!"

"Hahahahaha, Yeah and unless God writes me a letter to correct me, people who haven't been to church in years are showing up at Spirit Temple Pentecostal Church tomorrow."

I decided this search was a wild goose chase and that it was time for a meeting of masterminds to hatch a game plan to catch a killer and find the lottery ticket in one big sweep, "That unbelievable."

"I spoke to Reverend Graves and he told me people started camping out on the church parking lot a couple of hours ago," he continued, "Money may not grow on trees, but some people sure as heck think God's going rain money from heaven."

CHAPTER 43

Detective Virginia Breeze

After coming up empty handed at the salvage yard, I decided to that this free time to catch up on some snail mail at the office. Technically I work for the NSA, but only a few people are aware of it and I'd rather keep it that way for now. I would rather avoid speculation as to why I am here working undercover as a cop. I work out of the main administrative building of the St. Louis Police Department. It is now late Saturday afternoon and no matter when you enter the Public Safety Operations and Training Facility, it is always busy. Some people really are busy while others manage to stay busy looking busy. The St. Louis facility has been ranked number two in the United States because of the Training classroom that can accommodate almost ninety people and it is designed theater style. It has a fully equipped communications and emergency operations center, evidence processing and storage, high tech audio visual support systems that allow classrooms to provide a variety of training scenarios, but the best feature of all is the Hot Center with the communications patch consoles. I walked to the mailroom and the weekend dull looking guy name Charles was standing in front of a sorting machine when the eye pad scanned my retina.

As soon as the door open the aroma of burnt popcorn hit my nose and I saw the way he glanced at me out of the corner of his eye and asked, "What's up with you this afternoon?"

"Just doing a little paperwork," I said as I walked over to the row of mail boxes along the far wall. The building was less than two years old, yet it has too much of a worked to many hours, and needs to be repainted as well as cleaned up. I passed a desk with an open bag of smoking, hot and burnt popcorn spilling onto the desk. Despite the advancements in technology some people still send typed memos for the whole world to see instead of using inner office email, so I reached in and pulled out the stake of papers and quickly fanned though the stake and Charles said, "I have a package in the back for you, and give me a second and I'll get it for you?"

"You could have left it on my desk," I commented.

He said, "Not this. It came with special instructions. I asked Captain West to have you stop in."

"No problem," I said out of curiosity, "What could be so urgent?"

Charles walked across the room walks over to an encoded steel box that is attached to the wall and entered a set of numbers and the box automatically opened. I walked over to the shredder and turned it on and hand fed each memo into the crossed teeth, then turning off the machine. He walks over with a flat Federal Express envelope and a small electronic sign-in pad, "Just put thumb on the pad."

172

I looked at screen and saw a name and tracking number of the package and as soon as I pressed my thumb onto the screen my picture popped onto the screen and confirmed my identity. Charles handed me the enveloped and walked back to the mail sorting machine as I torn open the envelope. I told Charles, "That popcorn's stinking up the entire room."

"Sorry about that," he said.

I reached into the envelope, "It's empty!"

"Who would send an empty envelope," Charles asks.

I held the envelope open so Charles could see it, "Empty!"

Charles glances at the open envelope, "No. There's a small envelope in the package."

I looked inside the shipping envelope this time and so there is, "A small yellow envelope."

Charles watched closely as I pulled it out and read the on the envelope and pulled out the Lottery Ticket and I yelled, "HOLY SHIT!"

Charles asks, "What is it?"

It was the elusive lottery ticket and there is a Post-It Note stuck to the front of the Lottery Ticket that read,

This Lottery Ticket was in the Tithe and Offering Envelope that has the name of the person who placed the ticket in the collection plate.

I ran from the mailroom and as ran into Tom Johnson on my way out the door, "Out of my way!" Tom tried to stop me and take the ticket "Stop running in here!"

I pushed him out of my way and had he not gotten out of my way I sure I would have shot him dead on the spot, but Captain West came up and grabbed Tom from the back and slammed him against the wall and shouted, "Assaulting an officer?"

Tom yelled, "I'll have your job!"

Captain West shouted, "Maybe, but not today!" Captain West slapped a set of hand cuffs on Tom and dragged him down the hall into the booking room.

CHAPTER 44

Nichelle Graves

Detective Breeze is very suspicious of Shawn, but so was I when we first married. Shawn and I have known one another from childhood. I lost contact with him while he was in prison and when he finally got out, everyone notice a difference, including his mother. I suppose that was part of the reason she was placed in a sanitarium for the criminally insane after the death of the Elder Reverend Graves. Elder Graves died shortly after ordaining his son Shawn. Shawn has a yellow marker in his hand and his bible open outlining a section. He has a legal pad at his side with notes jotted halfway down the page. I begin flipping through a fashion magazine, and stopped at one of the pages and looks at the Hooded Chocolate Cotton-Blend Jersey Cardigan by Alexander Wang, "I'd look fabulous in this," I said to Shawn.

Shawn glances at the outfit, "Yes you would, but not in church."

With my lips curled in a sneer, "I go other places as well as church."

"You not wearing an outfit like that anywhere unless I'm with you," said Shawn."

"Never mind my wardrobe…you better be worried about Detective Breeze I said with a dash of tart sarcasm.

"God is my shield and my Fortress," replied Shawn as he leafed through the book of Psalms.

The time has come for me to present the most compelling argument I could, "A warrant is eminent and if she proves you're Eric Campbell-you go back to prison or even death row."

"Incidentally," added Shawn , "I'm probably not the only one under suspicion."

I closed my fashion magazine and looked dead at Shawn and asked, "Just what are you implying?"

He answered, "Beulah and you."

"That's a curious statement," I continued, "But if I were you I would be gone by morning." I turned on the television and a male reporter in front of Spirit Temple Pentecostal Christian Church, "The crowd has been camped out here all night after the discovery of the body of Director of the Gaming Commission, Tyrone Lane was discovered in the coffin of the late Raymond Murdock."

Shawn stopped what he was doing and watched and said, "Look at the crowd."

The Reporter walked up to a man in the crowd and asked, "Why is everyone gathered here tonight?"

"THE SECOND COMING DUDE!" the man laughs, "YOU DIDN'T KNOW?" The crowd laughs.

The reporter says, "It has been confirmed that the wife of Tyrone Lane, Kirsten Lane was found dead earlier from an apparent suicide."

The reporter at the news desk interrupts, "We need to switch to Rachael Russell at the Gaming Commission."

Rachael Russell a woman of about twenty three and she is chicly dressed in tight, black, Club Monaco pants with an oversized tie-dyed shirt with a long blue scarf and black ankle boots. She reports, "Alan Douglas has been appointed interim Director until his official conformation and according to a statement released earlier that there was a winner for the One Billion Dollar Multi-State Lottery Drawing, but the winner has not came forward."

Nichelle looks at Shawn and says, "That could have been us."

Shawn shook his head, "I'm glad that cursed ticket is out of here." Shawn turns off the television.

I leaned over to look at what section Shawn was reading with such intensity. I looked at he was looking at Psalm 90:8 of the Old King James version of the Bible.

Shawn closes his bible and says, "I'll be back later...I'll be in my prayer room if you need anything," then he walks out of the bedroom and closes the door behind himself.

My iPhone-5 rang and I looked at the caller-Id, and it says, unknown caller. She presses one of the buttons and turns the phone off.

Shawn returns to the bedroom and I am certain it is because my phone rang. He gets back in bed with the bible open to Psalm 90:8. I looked at him slightly sideways as though I was looking at the Devil, "I thought you were going to your prayer room?"

He glanced sideways at me, "I was, but some answers come faster than others," he said warmly as he kisses me goodnight, then reads Psalm 90:8 again, and leaves the Bible laying open on Psalm 90:8 between the two of us.

CHAPTER 45

Shatoya Quinn

I am glad to be out of ICU and together in a regular hospital room. We are doing better than anyone realizes even though Jade has left leg is in a cast and my left arm is in a cast. Jade asks, "I wonder what happened to our lottery ticket?"

"Girl, are you nuts? We stole that ticket off the body of a dead man in church," said Shatoya.

"It's not like he was going to cash it in," remarks Jade.

"Jade, you seen the news just like I did...a bunch of people done turned up dead, and someone tried to kill us over that ticket."

"I wished I knew what happened to that ticket," said Jade.

I said point blank, "Don't bring up that ticket again-that thing is bad luck."

Jade tries to get out of bed using crouches, "Where are you going?" I demand to know.

"Outta here...I'm going get back what the Devil stole from me," said Jade.

"Fool, get back in bed before they call the police," said Shatoya.

Jade hobbles to the closet to find her clothes, but the closet is empty, "Dang...what happen to my clothes?" She opens the closet next to it and it was empty.

"That's God trying to tell your stupid butt to stay in that bed."

Jade tells me, "No that's a sign from the devil that I need to call kayak and NaNa and have them bring us some clothes."

My bed is nearest to the door and I lean forward and peer down the hall, "Quick...get back in bed...here comes the nurse!"

"I'm calling Kayak and NaNa," said Jade.

"Anything's better than sneaking out in the middle of the night," commented Jade as the nurse enters the room.

The nurse, "Time for vitals and the RN will be around in a few minutes with your medication."

CHAPTER 46
Virginia Breeze - Liza's Dream

The day's events kept replaying themselves through Virginia mind the entire night, but finally she drifted off in a deep slumber. Her Rim sleep is interrupted by the screams of Liza, she rushed into Liza and Madison's room, and turned on the lights, and found her wrapped in her covers, kicking and screaming, "Grandma, Grandma, don't go!"

I rushed in Liza's room and sits down on the side of the bed to gently wake her up, "Honey wake up."

I cried, "It was a terrible dream."

"It was only a dream," I said.

Nadine comes to the door and looks in at Liza and Virginia and was about to walk away when Liza sees her and screams, "Grandma, Grandma! You're ok."

Nadine smiles and walks in and I jump out of bed to and gave Grandma a big hug and she asked, "What were you dreaming?"

Liza's screams awoke Madison down the hall and Madison came and stood in the doorway as I begin to tell them my dream, "In dreamt some shot and killed Grandma and we had to go live with Uncle Oliver and Aunt Eileen."

I tried to ease and console Liza, "It was only a dream."

By 7 A.M. I had finished dressing and was having coffee with Nadine in the kitchen. I knew this was the opportunity to talk to Nadine and discuss my plan. I got up to pour myself another cup of coffee and told Nadine, "I have the Lottery Ticket."

Nadine looked at me, "You're kidding me!"

I informed her, "Nope, I got it in the mail yesterday."

Nadine is happy to hear the news, "Now you can solve the Murdock Case."

I sat down at the table and sat my coffee cup down, "Not quite."

Immediately, Nadine knew something is fishy and she asks, "But there's a catch, so what is it?"

"The killer is still in the church and Ray Murdock was killed because Tyrone Lane had rigged the lottery," I paused, "And I want to use the ticket as bate to catch the killer."

Nadine drinks down the last few drops of coffee like she's taking a swig of Jack Daniels and sits the cup down on the table, "What does it have to do with me?"

Nadine can refused and I would have to change the plan a slight bit, but I continued to persuade her, "You want be in any danger and you'll be protected the entire time."

Nadine asks, "What's the catch?"

I reached into my jacket pocket that is hanging on the back of my chair and handed her a one dollar bill and folded in with the bill was the lottery ticket, "Just before you begin the morning collection...I need for you to plant the ticket in the church collection plate."

Nadine commented, "I'm glad you didn't ask me to walk in water and not get caught."

182

"I know I'm asking a lot," I said.

Nadine thought about it for a few seconds, "Don't let Liza dream come true."

"It was just a dream," I paused and thought, "All you have to do is put it in the plate like to do your regular tithe."

"I always put my tithe in an envelope in the plate," said Nadine.

"I guess so," said Nadine.

My iPhone rang and Nadine sat quietly at the table as I took the call from the Social Worker at the Hospital, and they called to inform me that Shatoya and Jade are out of ICU and that I could come and questioned them at any time, and to let the nurse in charge know if I need any special accommodations.

"Great," I said as I got up from the chair and put on my jacket.

Nadine's eyes are fixed upon me, "Shouldn't you be wearing your gun?"

"I am," said Virginia.

"Well, dog gone if I see it," said Nadine

Virginia laughs, "That's the idea."

Nadine says, "Okay," and gets up to pour herself another cup of coffee.

"Call me if you need anything," said Virginia as she heads toward the door.

"The girls will be fine," said Nadine.

Nadine reassures her, "Don't worry," as Virginia walks out of the door.

Virginia walks into the spacious lobby of the hospital and stops at the information desk, and asks the receptionist, "I need to know what room Shatoya and Jade Quinn are in?"

The male reception clerk says, "One moment and I'll find out."

He begins typing on the key board, and he looks strangely before responding, "That's strange."

Virginia takes a quick survey of the people in the lobby, and then turns back to the receptionist, "Is there a problem?"The receptionist keeps typing on the keyboard before he finally looks up at Virginia and instructs her to, "Go up to the 7th floor Nurse's station."

"Thank you," Virginia responds, and then walks away towards the two columns of elevators, a number of people wait to board the elevator.

The elevator bells rings and the arrow points up, Virginia walks onto the elevator as the reception desk clerk watch's the elevator door closes.

A hospital worker walks over to the reception desk…the male receptionist tells the female, "I'm glad she's gone."

"Who was that," she asks.

"That police officer from the television…she came here asking about those twins," said the receptionist.

"The two they found missing at six o'clock this morning?" she woman gasped.

In an effeminate voice, the male receptionist responds, "Yes, Girl."

The female says in a shocked, but whispered tone, "Oh…somebody's in trouble."

Virginia patiently rode the elevator as it stopped and people got off, and some got on and rode to the next floor. The elevator stopped on the sixth floor and everyone got off; however, an elderly woman in her eighties slowly navigator her way off the elevator and Virginia held the elevator door open with one hand, the old woman turns to Victoria, "You getting off?"

"No, I'm going up to the next floor," Victoria answered as she continued holding the door. The old woman looked up at the numbers above the door, and there are only six floors. The old woman smiled and waved, "Good luck as the elevator door closed."

The elevator door closed and Victoria looks up at the above column of numbers, and there are only six floors, "What in the…" the elevator seems to be going straight down without stopping on any floor. The elevator suddenly stops on the ground floor, and an automated voice on the elevator say, "Please exit to your left, and have a good day."

Virginia exited the elevator, and turned to her left and walked down the dark chilly hallway. There were numerous empty gurneys and wheelchairs lined along the wall. The only sound was the sound of Victoria's boots on the concrete floor, and she thought to herself, "That receptionist…"

She continued walking and a sign on the wall read, Please Turn Left. Virginia turned left, came to the dead end of a brick wall, and said aloud, "I can't believe this!"

Virginia turns around in long hallway and headed back in the direction she came from. As she got closer to the elevation, the bell, "Ding," sending a signal that someone was getting off. She thought to herself, "I don't know who it is, but you may as well stay on the elevator."

The elevator bell continued dinging, but the door failed to open. Virginia kept pressing the up arrow button to no avail, so she began looking around for the stairwell, but there were none. Without warning, the elevator door opened, and she stepped on and the door closed behind her.

The elevator went up to the next floor and the door opened, and an elevator technician was standing in the door when it opened, "This is the third time today…this elevator seems to have a mind of its own. "

She was back in the lobby where she started. Virginia headed in the direction of the information desk and there were a group of hospital Security Officers and a young business woman standing among them and they are gathered around the desk, some of them murmuring among themselves. The attendant sitting at the information desk rose to his feet, and said, "I'm so sorry, but you need the East Elevators," and he points in the direction of the fountain in the center of the lobby.

The business woman walked up to me and politely introduced herself, "I'm Maria Small and I am head of the Senior Nurse Manager, she smiled and asked me, "How may I help you?"

I nodded and showed my badge and answered, "I need to know the room number for Jade and Shatoya Quinn?"

The woman looked at one of the guards before she answered, "They were here, but they have apparently left."

"They left," I said and I pause for a second to keep my composure, "What do you mean they left? My words seemed to have disturbed Maria, but depending on her answer, it will only serve to make me more inquisitive and once I find a gap I will have her running all day for an answer.

"That is currently under investigation, but security tapes show the woman leaving with an unknown woman," said Maria.

I said, "We'll also be investigating and I will be in contact," and I walked away.

Melvina Page is caught in morning rush hour traffic on the MLK Bridge that crosses the Mississippi River going east. Shatoya is the passenger seat, and Jade is in the back seat fidgeting, "You need to hurry...we need to get out of sight," urged, Jade.

"I glad we took a pain shot before we left," said Shatoya.

Jade added, "This is going to hurt like the devil later, then what will we do?"

Malvina hops from lane to lane, "I'm doing the best I can," she answered, and I'm sure Mom has something you can take that will help.

Shatoya, Jade and Malvina have known one another from grade school, and although Malvina is as sweet as she can be will do anything for anyone in need of help, but it's been well established that she is not playing with quite a full deck, but Malvina's house is the only place no one would think to look for them or so they thought. When Melvina pulled into the driveway, Captain West and two squad cars pulled up directly behind them.

CHAPTER 47

Reverend Shawn Graves

I was on my way to the church, and decided to stop at a nearby coffee house for a cup and coffee and a cheese Danish. As usual, I took my notebook computer in the shop with me, and I was typing the eulogy for the double funeral for Tyrone and Kristen. I was in deep concentration and typing when, she came in, Dana Khan...Dr. Dana Khan. We have not seen one another since I married Nichelle nine years ago. Dana had pale golden hair, and fair skin and hazel eyes. Dana is the daughter of Nobel Prize Botanist, Dr. Virgil Khan. Virgil had three daughters, Grace, Amy and Dana. All his daughters have hazel eyes and fair skin.

Dana nodded at the server without saying a word and walks over to Shawn table. I quickly typed my last thoughts as they poured out of my soul and she came over to my table, "Reverend Graves," said Dana.

I looked up and pretended to be surprised when I saw her standing there in a low cut red dress with a split that begins at the hem with her brown hair flowing down her shoulders. She pulls her hair off her shoulder, and reveals her diamond stud earrings.

She tilted her head and smiles as I stood up, "Dana...wow!" In the back of my mind, I wished she were my wife rather than Nichelle, but when I married her it was until death do we part. Seeing Dana brought back memories and I decided perhaps she had finally forgiven me, but I was determined to keep it short and exit. Shawn knew better than to take a woman at face value. Too many women want me for my money and would turn his life and ministry more upside-down than it already is. They hug one another, "I never expected to run into you," said Dana.

"I can't believe this...what brings you here?" asks Shawn.

"I was called in to consult on a murder investigation," said Dana.

"You're a botanist, not a detective," jokes Shawn.

"Someone was poisoned," said Dana

"Poison...sounds interesting," responds Shawn.

"It involves some church murders," said Dana.

I looked at her with surprise and awe, and begin placing my computer in my bag. I closed my bible and she said, "Don't tell me it's your church?"

"I've got to go and it was nice seeing you again," I said.

"I had no idea-I'm so sorry," she said.

I glance at her and said, "Sure you are."

I quickly exited the coffee house wishing that I had went straight to church as I had planned and as I was about to get into my car, Tony Rome appeared without warning and said, "Looks like you're in a tight spot?"

190

"Everything's under control and God's going to work this out," I said.

"Detective Breeze is on to you and your exit is eminent and you go straight to prison," chuckled Tony.

I stopped and looked at Tony and said, "I know who I am and who God said that I am," I persisted.

Tony said bluntly, "At the moment it's not what God thinks, but man or rather Detective Breeze and at the moment she wants to prove that you are Eric Campbell not Shawn Graves."

I suddenly froze up and took off my glove and looked at my burnt hands fearfully, "I know who I am…"

He said, "Consider this option," he gazed at me, "Disappear right here and now."

"It would make sense until this has blown over," I suggested.

"You shouldn't have to hid, but why would you take the chance of being fingered as the killer of Murdock, Newton, Lane and his nutty wife and whomever else that may have been murdered over the past thirteen months," said Tony.

I looked glanced at the coffee shop and saw Dana sitting at table next to the front window watching Tony and I, "When do I do this Harry Houdini number?"

He answered, "Right now." An Indigo Blue Metallic Jaguar F-type with a jet black roof and twenty inch cyclone black wheels and red calipers speeds onto the parking lot and Tony opens the door and said, "Get in and don't look back and don't ask any questions."

191

I looked at the driver with complete shock and couldn't believe my eyes and she looked at me and smiled then looked at Tony. Tony looked around and saw Dana watching us and he said to me, "Stop staring and get in now."

CHAPTER 48

Dr. Dana Khan

At this moment I am experiencing the same feeling she had the day Shawn left me standing at the altar. I slowly sip my Mocha Cappuccino. People begin crowding the Coffee Shop and the man I saw talking to Shawn walks over to my table with a bagel and a large cup of coffee and asks, "Mind if I sit with you?"

I looked up at the man wearing a tan cargo shorts with a white dress shirt and jacket, and answered, "Of course not." But the truth is I did mind, but I was curious what he wanted from me and where Shawn went.

He sits down and takes a bite from his bagel, then says, "Excuse my manners. My name is Tony Rome." Tony looks around the Coffee Shop before looking Dana in the eyes.

Dana smiles, "I'm Dana Khan."

Tony looks me over while not trying to be obvious, "Dr. Dana Khan?"

I looked at him suspiciously, "Yes…as a matter of fact," I answered and then asked him sharply as though he was a paparazzi reporter, "Are you a reporter?"

Tony laughs, "What difference does it make? What if I were?"

I got up and walked out the door, "I don't have any comment," I told him as I walked out the door.

Tony walks out of the coffee shop and ran to catch up with me. I unlock my rental car door, and Tony caught up with me, "You had a lot to say to Reverend Shawn Graves a minute ago," I opened the car door and got in, but Tony prevented me from closing the door.

I forced a fake smile at Tony as a couple watches Tony from the window of the Coffee Shop then I snapped at him, "Yeah, what business is it of yours?"

"I just thought you'd like to know that the person that was poisoned is Shawn Graves' father-in-law, Ray Murdock. The victims are members of his church!" Tony closes her car door, "Have a nice day Dr. Khan," then he walks away.

I watched as Tony got into a solid black SUV and speeded away, but as soon as I pulled off the Coffee Shop parking lot an unmarked police car flash's its lights and I pull over to the shoulder, and reach's into my purse for my passport and international license, "What have I gotten into in the United States?"

A plain-clothes officer comes over to my car, and flashes her badge and Identification, but she flashed it so quick I hardly had time to read it, but I caught the name, "Detective Virginia Breeze, St. Louis Police Department." Virginia asks, "Dr. Dana Khan?"

Puzzled, "Yes I'm Dr. Dana Khan."

Two police cars pull up beside my car and I asked, "What's going on?"

Detective Breeze answered, "I need for you get out of the car and ride with me, and I'll explain."

I got nervous and concerned, "I have diplomatic immunity…I want to contact my embassy," I demanded.

A male officer opens my car door, "I'll drive your car." Dana grabs her purse and a leather portfolio and gets out of the car.

Virginia looks around, "Hurry. Get out of the open. You're not under arrest, but you are in danger."

Numerous police cars block off the street, and a police helicopter lands in the middle of the intersection of Skinker and Clayton Road, and Virginia grabs Dana by the arm, "Follow me."

The Police Officers help Dana and Virginia into the helicopter and like the invisible wind the helicopter slowly lifts off in an Easterly direction.

CHAPTER 49

Detective Virginia Breeze

It is early Sunday morning and the humidity has made the outdoors sweltering and the heat scorching. Captain Reed and I awakened Judge Perry Boone at 6 A.M. to get him to sign a court order that would allow us to take Reverend Shawn Graves in and examine his hands and fingerprint him for a comparison with the fingerprints of Eric Campbell. Captain Reed and I setup a secret sting operation within the church to track the Lottery Ticket once Nadine makes the drop in the collection place. We obtained a second warrant that would allow us to observe the Church Service activities from every angle via the media observatory.

The services had started by the time we arrived and to our surprise Reverend Graves was not there and the Spirit Temple Pentecostal Christian Church full to the fifty thousand seat capacity. There are three eighty-four foot Sony LED Television's suspended on the back wall of the stage. Most people refer to them as JumboTrons. There are cameras and lights suspended from the ceiling Yes, I said stage because it looks more like a concert stage than it does a pulpit of a church. The round, five hundred thousand square foot structure of the building looks more like a shopping mall than a church.

The Junkyard Prophet was preaching, "Have ever wanted to kill someone?" The congregation remained silent and he continued, "I'd better preach to myself?"

"Amen," yelled throughout the church by various people within the congregation.

"The Devil's been busy in the Spirit Temple Pentecostal Christian Church."

The crowd went silent again, and Junkyard raised his voice and is saying, "God said beauty for ashes, but by the Devil keeps giving us ashes to ashes!"

People started randomly yelling, "Hallelujah!"

People are seated in stadium style recliners and some are standing and others are walking in the isles, but we made our way through the church and to the Media Observatory. The door of the room was locked and there was no answer when we knocked. The large sign on the door read, DO NOT ENTER, but Captain West entered and two seven foot tall, Goliath Security guards immediately approached ready for battle with steel batons with razor sharp spikes circling around them, and they had one in each hand and I was ready to grab my gun and Captain West looked at me and said, "I got this!"

I showed my badge and the Court Orders, but they did not faze the two guards. The company is called Goliath Security because all the security guards look like Goliath's, but I and Captain West are no David's and I feel fine with putting a bullet in both of them. One of the guards raised his baton at Captain West and I pulled my revolver and said, "By his strips ye are healed, but by the bullet ye be dead!"

Both men dropped their weapons as two Uniformed Police Officers come into the Media Observatory and handcuffed both men, and Captain West instructed them, "Take them out the back way so no sees you!" The room was filled with television monitors that covered every angle of the church and The Junkyard Prophet. The various technicians had stopped what they were doing and were watching Captain West and I, and I said, "We are only here to observe," that relaxed the television crew a little and they got back to what they were doing.

One of the cameras zoomed in for a tight close-up shot of The Junkyard Prophet and the Female producer turned up the audio so we could hear Junkyard's sing song style hooping, "Sometime you have to give people to God and other people you have to lay down your Bible and send them to God!"

Captain West said, "He's got to be kidding with that crap."

Some of the monitors showed people dancing and shouting in the isles as the music producers gives the keyboard player playing instructions to match the rhythm of Junkyard and one of the technicians said, "People love it!"

Captain West commented, "That why this place stays packed?"

One of the overhead camera zoomed in on a woman dancing and shouting and a man is sprawled out on the floor having convulsions and the producer said, "Here's our boy-Johnny Holy-Ghost!"

One of the men jokes, "And he's right on queue!"

Junkyard continues, "It's done got quiet in here!"

More people started jumping and shouting like a bunch of church house zombie psycho's at a picnic. The Junkyard Prophet started preaching with greater enthusiasm, "The rope might be binding, but you'd better be care you don't hang yourself!" There was a brief pause for a few seconds before he continued, and said, "Read Isaiah 6:8," and the scripture appeared on the television screen and from memory he loudly quoted the scripture, "Also I heard a voice from the Lord, saying Whom shall I send and who shall go for us?"

A loud voice from the mist of the crowd yelled, "Here am I, send me!" The cinematographer ordered the camera operator to pan the camera around the crowd and try to get a shot of the man that yelled, but they are unable to find the exact seat and isle or the man had moved. The Junkyard Prophet is one of those preachers that is gifted with preaching and singing and as he walks to the center of the stage he grabs a microphone as the band starts playing. He starts singing the opening of Bishop Paul S. Morton's, Memorable Moments, that features, "*Don'tDo It Without Me.*"

As Junkyard and the choir sang the Church Usher's gathered for morning collection. Nadine was one of the Ushers.

They were lead in brief prayer by Mother Beulah then she gave each person a collection plate. Each Usher placed their tithe envelope in the collection plate including Nadine. I walked closer to the producer and told her, "Zoom in on the Ushers for a second," The camera zoomed in and I saw Nadine place the envelope in the collection plate.

We watched the entire collection process and for a big church it is very organized and we watched Nadine's collection plate go down the row. There the plate stopped moving when a Shatoya and Jade stopped to make change for a twenty from the loose currency in the collection plate. Captain West said, "Tell those chick's that is not a bank." Shatoya and Jade broke the twenty like Jesus broke bread and they put one dollar each in the collection plate.

"The producer said, "They do that all the time."

"I had no idea," observed Captain West.

It only took fifteen minutes from start to finish for complete the morning collection and we watched as the collection was taken to the counting room. The room and doors had been repaired and there is a new safe installed. The safe is the type owned and accessible only to armored car companies. The watched the finance committee members count the money with the precision of a professional bank tellers using automated counting machines. Another larger machine counted and wrapped the currency by denomination and fed in the safe. The tithing envelopes are placed in a neat pile and given to finance clerk and taken to Shatoya and Jade's office to process Monday morning.

Captain West and I watched the entire counting process. Since Ray and Tyrone were dead it didn't take long to replace them and they were replaced by Devine Prophetess Quinn and Magda. We watched as Nadine's envelope was opened by Magda and she showed it to The Prophetess and Mother Beulah. Beulah looked at the ticket and placed it back into the envelope and laid it on top of the pile. The idea of another ticket showing up in the collection plate was a joke to everyone, but Mother Beulah and Nichelle. We watched as Mother Beulah unlocked Shatoya and Jade's office placed the large box with all of the other tithe envelopes and locked them in the office.

Captain West and I made our way in the direction of the counting room because I needed to locate Shawn Graves. Nichelle was coming out of the counting room when we arrived. Nichelle looked dead at Captain West and demanded, "Why did you arrest my security detail?"

"Threatening a police officer with spiked clubs," replied Captain West.

Nichelle said sharply, "They were just doing their job."

I asked, "Their job is to beat people down with clubs?"

Nichelle looked at me and said, "Gun are not allowed in church, so we decided for safety sake that they could use spiked clubs."

I looked at her and ask, "I need to see Reverend Graves."

Nichelle asked, "Why?"

"We can only discuss it with Reverend Graves," I said.

"I'm his wife and you can tell me and I'll give him a message," she said.

Captain West asked, "Where is Shawn

Graves?"

I said, "Some would think you've got something to hide."

The church staff started filing out of the counting room and Nichelle whispered, "Shawn is preaching at a leadership conference in Atlanta."

"When will he be back," I asked.

Nichelle, "I think tonight."

Captain West looked at Nichelle and said, "He's your husband and all you've got is you think?"

I asked Nichelle, "What airline is he on?"

Nichelle said, "He never uses the airlines," and she smirked and continued, "He took our private plane to Atlanta."

I thought for a moment and asked, "What hanger do you used?

Nichelle answered, "Mid-America Airport."

If he filed a flight plan, they would have record of it, but for some reason I bet he didn't, but one phone and I verify my suspicions.

CHAPTER 50

Detective Virginia Breeze

Captain West and I had the entire setup planned to perfection. Christian Kane was to stake out the interior of the Lottery Office when the person arrived to collect the One Billion Dollar grand prize Lottery Ticket. And I showed the Lottery Director, John Marlin a copy of the ticket, "I need to verify whether or not this is a legitimate winner or not."

"I would like to be able to help you but there is a problem here," John cost for a moment or and looked at the photocopy of the front and back, "I don't have and all the information to help

Captain West sat and will high back chair with his legs crossed and he looked directly at Director Marlon, "She just gave you a perfect photocopy of the ticket, what else do you need to know?"

Christian is rubbing his hands together and contemplating his next move. He gets up from his seat and walks over to director Marlins desk and looks at the photocopy of the ticket, "and What's missing?"

Director Marlon opens his desk drawer and pulls out blank ticket and turns it over shows it to Christian and points to the serial number printed on the back of the ticket, "You see this serial number?"

Christian answered, "Yes I see it."

By this time both I and Captain West had walked over to Director Marlin's desk, we looked at ticket and we looked at the ticket and only saw a seven digit number and name of the issuing state, Missouri. Director Marlin turned to his computer terminal arrowed down to the Retail option then hit the return key. He waited a second, "I'm going to show what I can tell you about ticket," said Director Marlin. The next screen that popped up was box that he entered the serial number from the ticket. Instantly a data exploded across the screen and the director explains, "This information tells me what retailer was issued this roll of ticket stock and as you can see the system gave us another serial number."

I watched carefully as he arrowed over to the number and hit enter key again and like magic, the name of the retail location came up, "This looks like a small Mom and Pop store called Quinn's."

Captain West walked back to his chair and sat back down, "Yeah, I know the place."

I comment, "It's been in business a long time."

Director Marlin said, "The lottery license was issued to Louis Quinn."

"I knew him also," said Captain West.

I looked at Captain West and said, "You know him?"

"Used to go in there all the time before he died two years ago," said Captain West.

I walked back to my seat and sat next to Captain West, but Christian continued watching the Director.

The Director continued keying information on his computer, "That's strange."

Christian bent over and looked at the computer and pointed to a something on the screen, "Why does it say the license was renewed the week before the ticket was issue?"

"That's what so strange," Director Marlin paused and then continued, "The license was renewed by Louis Quinn a week before the date on the copy of the ticket." He exits from the screen and the system takes him to another State-wide database and he keys in the name Louis Quinn along with the Social Security Number. I went back to his desk and watched what came up and another a few moments, the death certificate of Louis J. Quinn with the date of death of January 13, 2010.

The Director pulls up another screen and a picture popped up in the screen and immediately I knew who it was, "I can't believe this."

Captain West walked over and looked at the screen and picture, "You've got to be kidding!"

The Director turned at Captain West, "What seems to be the problem?"

Captain West answered "That's not Louis Quinn."

Director Marlin tried to prove he was right, "We have a several checks and balances in place to identity people, so there are no mistakes."

"Well the lottery just bounced that check and the balance is off kilter," Captain West said firmly.

The Lottery Director got a little annoyed and said, "This is not supposed to happen," and he continued, "I intend to get to the bottom of this," and he points at the picture of the man on the screen and demanded, "Who is this?"

"His name is Alvin Carney," answered Christian.

I added, "Also known as, "The Junkyard Prophet.""

The Director got up from his desk and raised his voice, "I know you can't be talking about that television preacher?"

Captain West said with a hint of sarcasm in his voice, "The one, the only prophet on hand to share God's plan!"

The Director glared at Captain West as he informed him, "I want to the actual ticket."

I nodded at Captain West, "I'm sure you do," I murmured as Captain West and I left to get into position. Christian remained inside just in case something unforeseen should occur.

I have a team of twenty officers hidden and otherwise camouflaged at the St. Louis Lottery Office's gated parking lot. Even the guard at the main gate is one of Christian's men. Captain West and I waited in ordinary and a very plain looking van with an entire swat team. I still feel apprehensive because of what I have learned about the church I grew up in and the people Nadine and I knew.

I watched on the television monitor as a 2013 Hyundai Veloster Turbo stopped at the front gate and after a few seconds, the gate opened and the car drove in and parked near the entrance. I turned to one of the officers sitting at the console next to me and instructed him, "Run the plate."

The officer replied, "Doing it now," and after a momentary pause, he said, ""That plate does not go to that car."

Captain West asked, "Whose is it?"

"Tyrone Lane and it says he's deceased," the officer said.

We watched as the door on the driver's side of the Hyundai opened, and we were stunned by whom we saw get out of the car and Captain West yelled, "No way!"

I said, "This is not right!" I sent a signal to Christian via his iPhone, "He's on his way in."

Christian responded, "This is unbelievable."

Even as Christian paused I could hear him frowning, "This kid?"

"Yes, Troy Mosley," I said.

ABOUT THE AUTHOR

Kathy Bobo is a graduate of Columbia College, Columbia. She is the author of, *The Gospel According to Lucifer*, screenplay, *Warden's Lullaby and Secret Sin: Murder in the Church. Kathy lives in St. Louis, Missouri.* You can visit her on the web at www.kathybobo.webs.com, Facebook and Twitter.

www.ingramcontent.com/pod-product-compliance
Lightning Source LLC
Chambersburg PA
CBHW060807120626
46557CB00001B/116